C

Red River Raiders

For ten months it had not rained over the famed Bar 10 cattle ranch. With everything tinder dry, a fire was inevitable. Soon the entire eastern side of the huge ranch was engulfed in flames forcing Gene Adams and his trusty riders, Tomahawk and Johnny Puma, to seek help in the notorious Red River valley.

But unknown to the riders of the Bar 10, an evil force had been hired by the enemies of Adams to take over the vast ranch. The dozen ruthless horsemen knew that the raging fire, which was keeping Gene Adams and his men occupied, was the perfect time for them to strike. The Bar 10 was the prize and the invading riders were the Red River Raiders.

In this gripping tale it is always in doubt whether, after all the fire and blood, justice can prevail.

Red River Raiders

Boyd Cassidy

A Black Horse Western

ROBERT HALE · LONDON

ISBN 0 7090 7223 6

Robert Hale Limited
Clerkenwell House
Clerkenwell Green
London EC1R 0HT

Typeset by
Derek Doyle & Associates in Liverpool.
Printed and bound in Great Britain by
Antony Rowe Limited, Wiltshire

Dedicated with thanks to the great cowboy star,
Dale Roberston

PROLOGUE

The Bar 10 had grown over the years. Like a tiny acorn turning into a massive oak-tree, the ranch had become more than just a place where the best long-horn cattle in Texas were bred. It had become turned into a million acres of the best-kept land in all of the Lone Star state.

When Gene Lon Adams had first arrived more than forty years earlier, it was a beautiful land, but raw. It had taken the vision of one man to mould it into a living entity that could sustain up to ten thousand head of prime longhorn steers on its lush pastures and ranges. Up to fifty cowboys worked within the boundaries of the largest cattle spread in Texas, maintaining a balance that even nature could never have equalled.

Adams did not just have a vision for what the Bar 10 could and would become, he also had the strength of character to implement his dreams. He protected and fought for what he knew was right. He had never crossed anyone in a deal and would not allow anyone to do so to him.

Simple rules which, like the man himself, had stood the test of time. Adams had lost count of how many times he had been forced to strap on his gunbelt with its matched pair of golden Colt .45s to protect what belonged to him.

Yet he had never once fired those guns if it were possible to resolve his problems another way.

Four decades had seen the massive Bar 10 grow into a living creature which had survived everything men and nature had thrown at it.

Everything that is, except drought.

For the first time since Gene Adams had arrived with his prime longhorn breeding stock and an ancient-looking companion known only as Tomahawk, the elements seemed to be challenging his very right of guardianship.

Cloudless blue skies and a blazing hot sun were a beautiful sight for anyone to behold, but without rainfall in almost an entire year, even the strongest of things start to wither and die.

Gene Adams's million-acre empire of so many diverse qualities was being starved of the one thing all living entities require to exist.

Water!

The Bar 10 was literally dying of thirst.

ONE

It was hotter than the bowels of Hell itself along the parched Texan landscape as the three horsemen galloped across its arid stone-hard ground. For over three hours the riders had driven their faithful mounts continually onward without pausing for even a moment's rest.

There was an urgency in the gloved hands of the three cowboys as they continued to slap the long reins across the shoulders of their lathered-up mounts: a steely determination found only in men who came from the famed Bar 10 ranch as they thundered into the shimmering heat haze.

It was not the first time that Gene Lon Adams had led the way atop his chestnut mare with Johnny Puma and the wily Tomahawk in close pursuit. Yet with sweat burning his dust-caked eyes, he knew it might just be the last.

There had been no clouds in the vivid blue sky over Adams's massive cattle empire for nearly ten months. Across its million acres, not one single drop of rainwater had fallen for all of that time. Like all

9

living things deprived of the precious gift of water, it was dying.

The Bar 10 had suffered severe droughts before in its long forty-year existence, but had survived them all. Yet the last had been long ago, when there were fewer of the massive beeves roaming its ranges requiring fresh grass and water.

This drought was different.

There was no mercy in this one. It was as if the Lord himself had forsaken the vast cattle ranches and allowed Satan to do his worst.

The chest-high lush grass that covered at least three-quarters of the Bar 10 had grown dangerously dry over the past few months and no longer swayed in the Texan breeze. Now it just snapped like the kindling it had become.

Its forested eastern boundaries had become equally parched beneath the cruel sun that dragged every ounce of moisture from it. What did not perish under the blazing golden orb, was now being consumed by deadly flames.

Flames that had been created by the very heavens above and yet seemed more fitting to belong in Hell itself. Flames that had risen like a demonic creature bent on destroying everything in its path.

Even a million acres was not big enough to quench the insatiable hunger of a fire that had started in the pine forests and was now racing unchecked across the vast pasture land of the Bar 10.

Gene Adams had read the signs well at first. He had known it would be only a matter of time before the very land itself would ignite once every drop of moisture had been sucked from its trees and grass.

Yet even Adams had been shocked at the speed and size of the wall of flames that had met his eyes that very same morning. It had been as if the entire eastern section of his beloved Bar 10 ranch had been turned into a hundred-feet-tall fire that stretched from one horizon to the next.

He had seen fires before but nothing like this one. This blaze was eating up the dry land before it at an incredible rate. It was moving fast.

Too damn fast!

Adams had sent all thirty of his wranglers to try and fight the blaze as it destroyed everything in its path. The men would not quit whilst there was breath in their bodies but Adams knew that cowboys were no match for the fury of nature itself. All they could do was, he hoped, slow it up a tad.

Buy him and his two closest friends a little time.

Time that Gene Adams prayed would allow him to find the solution to this seemingly impossible situation. Yet as the white-haired rancher drove his exhausted chestnut mare on and on with the black quarter horse and pinto keeping pace behind him, he knew this was no mortal enemy he had to fight this time.

The rancher had never met a living man he could not defeat but how could you fight the wrath of nature when it was hell-bent on destroying everything that lay in its way?

But he had to try.

Gene Adams was not a man who quit easily. It was not his way. Riding through his beloved Bar 10 he had seen the powerful destructive forces he was attempting to defeat. A ten-month drought had brought nothing but death to his stock. Adams had lost count of how many of his prime longhorn cattle he had seen lying twisted on the sun-baked ground that morning.

Death had already sunk its claws into the Bar 10.

A death caused by dry water holes.

The Bar 10 itself was dying.

Months earlier, Adams had sold off half his stock when it became obvious his massive ranch could no longer provide the herds with enough food or water. Yet there were still at least five thousand more longhorns out there and they were dying.

Five thousand steers which had stampeded in every direction when the first flames had leapt from the pine forests and ignited the tall dry grassland. They had already been half-loco due to lack of water but now they also had the stench of the burning inferno in their wide nostrils.

After forty years of fighting the elements and everything else that got in his way, Gene Adams could not easily accept that this was a battle he could possibly lose.

Yet even twenty miles from the wall of fire which was forging its way relentlessly into the heart of Adams's huge cattle ranch, the riders too could still smell the acrid smoke.

Adams whipped his long reins from one side of his

galloping horse to the other, leading his faithful friends towards a destination that he prayed might just hold the answers.

Adams had never been faced with anything like this before and fretted that he was not actually heading towards a place that would provide a salvation for the Bar 10, but in truth, he was simply running away from his inevitable destiny.

Tomahawk and Johnny Puma followed Gene Adams as they had always done. Neither rider had ever questioned the tall rancher because he was a man unlike any other man they had ever had the privilege of knowing. Wherever Adams went, they dutifully followed.

He led and they followed.

Gene Lon Adams stood in his stirrups and rode on. He had to find a way of stopping this nightmare whilst there was still enough time to do so.

The trouble was, he doubted that even God had the power to stop the fire which was engulfing the Bar 10.

TWO

At last Gene Adams heeded the frantic pleas of his
two best friends and dragged his reins up to his wide
chest. A cloud of dry fine dust seemed to plume into
the air as the hoofs of the tall horse obeyed its
master's command. The chestnut mare staggered to
a halt as the two other riders stopped their own
mounts next to the grim-faced rancher.

For a few seemingly endless moments none of the
three said anything. Their eyes surveyed the familiar
landscape as if they had never seen it before.
Perhaps it was the acrid smoke that filtered even
here on the hot air that made everything appear
different. It could have been the sound of exploding
trees far behind them in the pine forests or even the
way that it spooked their mounts which made the
trio of horsemen so silent. Whatever it was, it was
real.

As real as the sweat that soaked their shirts
beneath the hot sun and blinded their eyes with
dazzling reflections off the white ground.

'I thought you was never gonna stop, Gene,' Tomahawk gasped as he slid from his saddle and collapsed on to the hard ground. Every bone in his ancient body hurt.

The youthful Johnny Puma said nothing. He tossed his right leg over the neck of his pinto pony and dropped on to the ground. For the first time in his life, he was afraid. Resting his gloved hands on the grips of his matched Colt .45s he looked back at where they had come from. The smoke made it impossible to make out any of its landmarks. He was an expert with his guns but knew this was a skill that could not resolve what was happening to the Bar 10.

Gene Adams dismounted reluctantly and stared at their horses before shaking his head.

'I reckon I must have been half-loco to push these poor critters so hard without a rest, boys,' he admitted.

'I'll water them, Gene,' Johnny said, lifting his canteen off his saddle horn and staring at the black smoke-filled sky behind them.

Adams watched as the youngster poured water into his Stetson before carefully placing it on the ground beneath the nose of the pony. The tall rancher removed his own ten-gallon hat and handed it to the quiet cowboy. Both men nodded silently at one another. After so many years, they could almost read each other's thoughts.

'I don't figure that fire will reach the centre of the Bar 10, Gene.' Tomahawk sighed. He got to his feet and tossed his battered hat on to the ground. 'After

all, with the water hole dab-centre next to the
bunkhouse and corrals . . .'

'Stop it, old-timer,' Gene Adams muttered looking
back at the black sky and the flames which snaked
heavenward. 'The water hole is nearly dry and you
know it. That fire will just walk right over the Bar 10
courtyard if it reaches there. A handful of wooden
buildings will be black cinders before you can muster
spit.'

'The boys will slow it up,' Tomahawk said in a voice
that held no conviction in it. 'They've fought fires
before.'

'Not like this one.'

Johnny Puma poured the last of the water into
Tomahawk's upturned hat and replaced the stopper.

'Ain't you got an opinion, Johnny?' Adams asked
as he watched his brooding young friend hanging
the canteen back on the saddle horn. 'Ain't you
gonna put in your two cents' worth?'

Johnny rested his back against his pony and
exhaled.

'How come we can still smell that damn fire, Gene.
It don't figure we ought to be able to still smell it.
We're upwind of it for heaven's sake.'

Tomahawk patted the shoulder of the lean
cowboy.

'The smell is in ya nose, boy. We done sucked in a
ton of smoke before we lit out with Gene.'

Johnny nodded. 'Reckon so. I'm kinda jumpy, I
guess.'

Adams rubbed his face.

'We better take the saddles off these horses. They're shot and need at least an hour's rest.'

'I got me some oats in my saddle-bag, Gene,' Tomahawk piped up.

Adams stared straight at the older man.

'Good. You can feed them after we take these saddles off their backs.'

'But the fire, Gene.' Johnny pointed a gloved finger at the distant smoke and flames. 'Can we afford to just sit around for an hour or so?'

'I don't know, Johnny. But if'n we don't, these horses will fold up underneath us for sure. We still got a long ways to go.'

'Where are we headed, Gene?' Johnny asked anxiously.

'The Red River,' Adams said, lifting the fender of his saddle and hooking its stirrup over the saddle horn.

'But why?' Johnny asked again.

Tomahawk held on to the sleeve of the younger cowboy and led him to their own horses. Their eyes met.

'Hush up,' Tomahawk whispered.

Nothing more was said.

THREE

It was a little more than an hour later when Happy Summers and Rip Calloway drove their horses across the almost bleached ground at a pace both men knew was too fast in the afternoon sun. Yet they had spotted the familiar sight of Gene Adams and his two companions far below them from their high vantage point on the western ridge, and wanted to find out what the rancher was doing so far away from the heart of the Bar 10.

Both cowboys had watched helplessly as the distant fire had grown and spread during the hours of daylight. Neither man knowing what they ought to do, they had done nothing. What would Gene Adams want them to do?

They had considered riding back to the centre of the Bar 10 to see if they could help. They had been about to do just that when they spotted the familiar trio of riders astride their equally distinctive horses, moving up the western trail towards them.

It seemed strange to the pair of skilled wranglers that Adams, Tomahawk and Johnny Puma would be so far away from the raging inferno that was eating up the ranch. Yet both riders knew that there had to be a very sound reason for their being here and not there.

The Bar 10 had four identical outposts dotted around its boundaries which were always manned by two cowboys in each line hack. It was their jobs to tend the cattle in their sections ands also keep an eye out for trouble. They would spend a month living and working at the isolated shacks before being replaced by fresh cowboys.

Adams had learned long ago that a month was about all men could tolerate before going loco.

A million acres of land required more than just four such remote outposts but even the Bar 10 had to draw the line somewhere. Adams knew that even if he had a cowboy placed two or three hundred yards apart around his vast ranch, it still would not be enough to protect the Bar 10 from anyone determined to try their luck.

Happy Summers and Rip Calloway rode their cutting horses down the dusty incline, then reined in when they reached the three seated men.

Gene Adams pushed the wide black brim of his ten-gallon hat back off his tanned face and stared up at the two dismounting cowboys. The rancher knew they were like the rest of his Bar 10 ranch hands and expected him to have all the answers. He wished that were true.

'I wondered when you two boys would get here.' The rancher touched the brim of his hat in greeting.

'That fire is eating up ground faster than a hog at supper-time, Gene,' Happy Summers said frantically. 'Me and Rip have been watching it all day wondering what to do. We didn't know whether to return to the ranch house or stay here.'

'Then we spotted you heading up through the pass,' Calloway added.

Adams's eyes glanced over his two best friends seated on the hard ground beside him, then looked back up at the two rannies.

'You did right by staying at your post, boys.'

'We had a couple of hundred head of longhorns stampede up over the ridge just after dawn. Reckon the smoke kinda spooked them. They just kept on running over the ridge and down on to the open range, Gene,' Rip Calloway said, nodding in the direction he meant.

'Makes no difference, Rip.' Adams sighed, got to his feet and dusted off his clothes. 'They're safer out on the open range than here on the Bar 10.'

'We can always round the critters up once this fire is out and bring 'em back, Gene.' Tomahawk sniffed, trying vainly to get back up off the hard ground.

Adams offered his gloved hands to his pal. 'If there's anything left to bring them back to, Tomahawk. Longhorns can't eat ashes.'

Tomahawk grabbed on to the rancher's gloved hands and pulled himself up off the hard ground. He was stiff and feeling as old as he looked.

'The boys will put that fire out darn soon, Gene.'

Adams raised an eyebrow but said nothing.

Tomahawk ran his tongue across his whiskered upper lip and turned toward Rip and Happy. 'Could ya see the boys fighting the fire from up there on the ridge, Happy?' the old-timer asked, trying to change the mood.

Happy Summers shrugged. 'Nope. All you can see is smoke and flames, Tomahawk.'

Johnny Puma rose to his full height, walked towards the three rested horses and scooped his blanket off the ground. He tossed it over the back of the pinto pony, patted it down then turned towards his saddle lying in the dust.

Gene Adams patted Tomahawk on his bony back. Dust rose into the air.

'Help the young 'un saddle the horses, Tomahawk.'

The old cowboy leaned close to the tall rancher. 'I don't like the way Johnny's brooding, Gene. Ain't healthy to bottle up your feelings like that.'

'You could be right, Tomahawk.' Adams tugged at his white beard and somehow managed to smile. 'Now go and help him saddle up our mounts before I pop my cork.'

Rip Calloway rubbed trail dust from his face.

'Where are you boys headed, Gene?'

'The Red River, son,' Adams replied bluntly.

'Why there, Gene?' Happy bit his lip.

'I got me an idea.'

'Is it a good 'un?'

Adams sighed heavily.

'It better be, 'coz it's the only one I've got.'

FOUR

Red River was a small twenty-building town sitting on the banks of the river of the same name. It was a place Gene Adams avoided like the plague for many reasons. The main one was because the people who occupied the town and the ranges that surrounded it, hated his guts.

Not that Adams had ever done anything to any of them except own a cattle ranch which was bigger than all those dotted around the seemingly endless range with the muddy river flowing through its centre combined.

Yet to most, that was enough.

The open range seemed to go on for as far as the eye could see. There were mountains off in the distance but few had ventured in their direction, so it was impossible to know how far away they actually were. Not that it mattered because the almost flat land of the range was big enough to cope with the scores of individual homesteads situated upon its fertile soil.

　　　　　Red River Raiders

Red River the town survived because of the river and the countless small ranches that used the range to fatten and water their stock. There was plenty of scope in the town for the men of business to live in grand style off the backs of the hard-working souls who raised cattle. For Red River was the only town within a hundred miles and capitalized on that fact. The saloons and gambling-halls knew that the surrounding ranchers would never dare cross the Bar 10 to try and reach a closer town.

Yet for some of the businessmen, even this was not enough to satisfy their natural appetite. Simply knowing of the massive Bar 10 ranch lying just beyond the white rock ridge was a temptation some could not resist.

Myths had grown in the minds of the most greedy who operated within the Red River township concerning Gene Adams and his reputed wealth.

Men who wanted more, knew exactly where it might be obtained.

For them just knowing one man controlled the largest ranch in Texas was too much to bear. They wanted their share of that priceless jewel. And plans to get their hands on some of that wealth were already being put into action.

The Bar 10 was just too tempting. Too many tall tales had grown around the famed cattle ranch that lay just over the ridge, to be ignored by those who existed solely to indulge their own perverse greed.

It was better land than the open range. Its long-horns always fetched bigger prices up in McCoy and other cattle towns than those raised around the Red River.

Four decades earlier Gene Adams and Tomahawk had travelled along the Red River and through its fertile ranges, eventually stopping when they discovered the land which they would later christen simply, the Bar 10.

Red River had grown more slowly than its prosperous neighbour with no single determined master at its helm, but the drought had evened things out over the past year.

Now Red River had something that Gene Adams wanted or needed if he was to execute his vague plan. Yet he did not relish riding down into the range he had grown to be wary of.

This was a place where the Bar 10 cowboys seldom visited unless they were looking for stray longhorns that had wandered off their ranch. For they knew that Red River and the lush ranges that surrounded it was the poor relation of Gene Adams's cattle empire.

Adams and his men had never been made welcome there. The rancher had once joked that every cowboy living in or around the Red River had green eyes.

Green with jealousy.

For forty years Adams had deliberately avoided contact with the men who rode those ranges unless it was vitally important that he do so. Blood had been spilled the last time Adams had entered Red River.

Reluctant to risk the lives of his loyal cowboys

Adams had chosen to trade with other towns to the north or east. But that was before the fire; the fire which had made it virtually impossible for him to reach anywhere except the Red River township.

It was a cautious Gene Lon Adams who led the four Bar 10 riders over the sun-bleached ridge and passed the line shack that identified the unmarked western boundary of his ranch.

For the first time in twenty-five years, Adams was entering a place where he knew he was not welcome. A place that the law had steered clear of for obvious reasons. A place where he had been forced to use his golden Colt .45s simply to get out alive the last time he had ventured into it.

The riders of the Bar 10 rode slowly down on to the Red River range.

FIVE

There was nothing unusual in seeing a dozen dust-caked riders out on the vast ranges which bordered with the western edges of the Bar 10 ranch. A score of smaller cattle ranches shared the normally fertile grasslands and cowboys roamed its seemingly endless pastures continuously.

Yet these riders were no ordinary cowboys sitting astride their lean well-trained mounts as they rode in single file along the river's edge.

They did not belong to any of the scores of ranches, or anywhere else within a hundred miles of the Red River township for that matter. Only a few of the infamous town's businessmen even knew of the dozen riders' imminent arrival and they had paid well for the service they guaranteed.

The skilful horsemen did know a lot about cattle, though. Other folks' cattle, that was.

The twelve riders had come from the north, from a place where the mighty Red River was nowhere near as wide or unpredictable as it was as it flowed through the massive open ranges near the town of the same name.

These men had never been simply cowboys or wranglers. They were however experts with all sorts of steers, whether they be longhorn, whiteface or crossbreeds.

Yet they were not simply rustlers either.

They had progressed far beyond that during the handful of years that they had been together working along the wide turbulent river. Mere rustlers just stole other people's cattle and then sold them for profit. These men worked for those who could afford their price, and their price was high.

The twelve horsemen who trailed along the banks of the Red River heading towards the town they had been summoned to, were far more dangerous than ordinary cattle thieves.

Each had honed his skills not just with a cutting rope and bullwhip for the steers they would rustle, but also with the guns they wore on their hips, guns they used ruthlessly without a second thought.

Each of the dozen riders had mastered the art of killing in cold blood for money. There were some who considered bounty hunters the lowest form of life in the West but at least they hunted those who were wanted by the law for crimes against humanity. The dozen riders killed anyone they were paid to kill, however innocent they might be.

Death had its price in a way that most civilized souls would never have considered possible. Yet these riders had earned their dubious reputations for being able to provide that service, with no questions asked.

They raided ranches and stole the herds they had been commissioned to steal. They did other men's dirty work without ever allowing human emotions to hinder their actions. They also killed every man, woman or even child who got in their way, or who had been marked out by their paymasters, for execution.

Whatever the reason that drove these creatures in human form ever onward, they continued to ride their chosen path without any thought for what they had left in their wake. They would carry on dishing out their own brand of death and destruction like a well-oiled machine for those who paid their fee.

Their names were, Billy Bob Smith and his three younger brothers, Joey, Caleb and Kermit. They had never known anything but stealing and killing and were the worst of the ruthless bunch. Mason Pyle, with flashing eyes and a mouthful of chewing tobacco, tailed the four Smiths atop a sturdy grey. He chewed and spat and seldom said a word. Porter Bruce and his cousin Elmer followed Pyle. They too chewed but also cursed continuously as they rode. Thaddeus Nelson had but one good eye and was said never to be known to blink. He had been known for his temper and drinking long before he hitched up with the Smiths. Broncho Bates was big – at least six foot three inches in height and 250 pounds in weight – but deceptively fast. He had been known to have once raced after a galloping horse, catch it and break its neck. None of the other riders ever crossed Bates. The rider who spurred his horse after the massive man was called simply Waco. Although he had ridden with the Smith brothers for more than a decade, nobody seemed to know anything about him. Waco was not a man to brag. All they knew for certain was that he was as deadly as a rattler. The last two riders, who ate the dust of the others, were a strange pair who never seemed to be far from one another. Their names were Tom Hetty and Silas Jackson. They had a bond that nobody could ever fathom and few questioned. All the other ten riders knew for sure was that if you wanted to die quickly, all you had to do was try and get between Hetty and Jackson.

These twelve dust-covered riders resembled ghosts as they followed the river towards their destination. But they were not ghosts, they were the infamous Red River Raiders.

SIX

The streets of Red River were seldom completely empty of cowboys and managed to stay open for their business twenty-four hours a day. There was absolutely nothing the small town could or would not provide for the ranch hands when they drifted through its drab streets.

It had never been a handsome town by anyone's standards, but then it had never been required to be so because it was the only one close enough for the ranchers and their cowboys to frequent.

Everything the ranches or their people needed was shipped in by wagon train regularly and the size-able profit added to the costs, made the small town one of the richest anywhere in the Lone Star state.

Red River had a captive clientele and the men who controlled it, knew so. Cowboys starved of even life's most basic luxuries had to spend their wages here. Yet Red River provided everything that their imaginations could envisage including the charms of female companionship. The things they wanted or craved were all here, for a price. The men who ran

Red River knew that the customers would always pay that price.

It was as if Red River had crammed in every sort of vice known to man within its few streets. Not an inch of space was wasted by those who controlled the town.

Few of its wooden buildings were exclusively used as dwelling places and most had more than one business operating from within its walls. At least four brothels existed either above or behind other stores. The barber shop had a bathhouse at its rear and an opium den run by two handsome Chinese females above. Even in one of the most isolated parts of Texas it was possible for those who wished to fill their minds with the powerful oriental clouds of self-delusion, to do so.

A large gambling-hall boasted of never once closing its doors in the twenty-odd years since it had been built.

As well as two well-furnished saloons within spitting-distance of each other, there were numerous smaller drinking-holes hiding in dark alleys or over legitimate business establishments.

Yet for all its diversity, Red River was in fact owned by only three men.

The oldest was a man named Jake Hooper. He had been in Red River when the first of its score of buildings had been erected and never allowed a single day to pass without telling at least one person of that glorious day. The second man was Kevin McCall. He had brought two wagons filled with beautiful females to the isolated town ten years earlier and acted as their agent in exchange for a sort of protection. All this for a mere fifty per cent of their labours. Over the decade during which he had run every brothel in Red River, McCall had become extremely rich. But it was the third man, Matt Francis who was by far the wealthiest of the prosperous trio.

He had decided not only to run the gambling-parlours but also buy the mortgages from most of the smaller businesses dotted around the small town. By installing cots in the storerooms of the various buildings the original owners were able not only to remain in gainful employment but to stay in Red River.

By adding a rudimentary bank to his financial portfolio, Matt Francis had soon managed to grow even wealthier than his two longer-established associates. Creaming off a percentage of their massive savings by seemingly legal bank charges, Francis had seen his own personal wealth blossom to a level that Hooper and McCall could never have imagined possible.

Yet even this was not enough for Matt Francis.

He knew there was an even bigger prize waiting for the right man to focus his sights upon.

He had known about the Bar 10 ranch ever since he'd first arrived on the lush Red River ranges and surveyed its vast grazing land. The stories of the richest cattle ranch in all of Texas had driven him into an almost insane desire to one day own that. The knowledge that it lay just over the white sun-bleached ridge of arid rock to the east of the town had become so tormenting, Francis had decided to act.

He enlisted the agreement of Jake Hooper and Kevin McCall that he should use their ample savings deposited in his bank (though not any of his own money), and had eventually mustered the courage to seek out and find Billy Bob Smith and the rest of the Red River Raiders.

A chance meeting between Billy Bob and Francis a few years earlier had remained in the memory of the businessman. For years he had secretly toyed with the idea of hiring the ruthless gang to attack the Bar 10.

A few months earlier he had taken that fateful step.

It had been an expensive exercise but with careful bookkeeping, Francis had managed to pay the massive sum demanded by the notorious gang without actually using a penny of his own incalculable wealth.

Francis had convinced his two less ambitious associates that it was possible to strike out at the Bar 10 ranch and live to tell the tale. Yet, unlike Jake Hooper, he had never met Gene Adams. To him the name was no more real than that of the legendary El Dorado.

Why should he fear Gene Adams? After so many years Matt Francis had simply assumed that the rancher must be so old by now that he was ripe for harvest.

It was a logical yet mistaken assumption.

SEVEN

Gene Adams pulled back on his reins and slowed his chestnut mare until it stopped. The rancher sat atop his tall lathered-up mount in the centre of the five riders. The lights of the distant town now edged out across the flat land as darkness slowly enveloped the fertile pastures. There was still at least an hour before the red glowing sun would disappear completely but Adams knew it would take far longer than that to reach Red River.

His eyes were focused on the town where it lay on the banks of the Red River. It looked so peaceful there even to one who knew better. Adams still remembered the last time he had visited that town and the bloodshed which had ensued. He had lost two men that fateful day and knew his golden guns had claimed the lives of at least three times that number.

He did not want a repeat of that horrific day, yet every sinew of his aching body knew that the odds on their getting in and out of Red River without a fight were long.

Long black shadows were cast across the vast range below them. The lights of numerous ranch houses could be seen dotted across the cattle-filled grazing land that lay before the five horsemen, like dozens of angry fireflies marking out their territory.

Adams gave a fleeting glance at the low sun before returning his attention once more to the small array of buildings. Pulling the black leather gloves tight over his hands he cleared his throat.

'There it is, boys. Red River.'

'It don't look much from here,' Rip Calloway observed. He unscrewed the stopper of his canteen and took a long swallow.

Happy Summers reached into his vest pocket and pulled out his tobacco-pouch. 'I figured it would be bigger by all the stories I've heard, Gene.'

'It's big enough, Happy,' Adams said. He accepted the canteen from Rip and took a sip of the warm water.

'Tell me, Gene. Why in tarnation are we heading to Red River in the first place?' Tomahawk asked as he stroked the palm of his right hand across the blade of the Indian axe tucked in his belt. An axe he had become so expert with over the years that it had become part of the man himself.

'Yeah, Gene,' Johnny joined in. 'How come we are going there? You always told me and the boys that Red River was off limits to the Bar 10.'

Adams sighed.

'We are going there because we can't get to any of the towns we normally use, boys. We have to buy us some provisions. Some mighty important provisions.'

'What good will that do the Bar 10?' Happy Summers leaned back against the cantle of his saddle and watched the others while his nimble fingers and thumbs rolled a cigarette.

'The only thing the Bar 10 needs right now is a whole heap of water to put out that fire.' Tomahawk shook his head as he spoke and thought about the inferno behind them over the ridge. 'Is you going to buy water?'

Happy Summers struck a match across his saddle horn, cupped the flame in the palm of his hands and sucked it into the twisted cigarette. Smoke drifted through his teeth as he spoke.

'I figure it would take that entire river to put out the fire back on the Bar 10, Tomahawk.'

'I'd buy that river if'n it was possible to move it back to our spread, old-timer.' Gene Adams patted Tomahawk's shoulder. 'Red River has got something we need to fight that fire, boys.'

'But what except water could we possibly need from down there that will help us fight the fire back on the ranch, Gene?' Johnny swallowed hard.

'It ain't water I'm heading there for, Johnny.' Adams lifted his Stetson off his face and ran his sleeve across his brow, then returned the hat to his head. 'We're gonna buy us a whole heap of dyna-mite.'

'Dynamite?' Tomahawk sat bolt upright in his saddle and turned to look at the tanned face of the rancher. 'Did you say dynamite?'

'You heard right, Tomahawk.' Adams confirmed. 'Dynamite!'

'Dynamite? What the heck do we want a whole passel of dynamite for, Gene?' Tomahawk scratched his beard feverishly.

There was the hint of a smile on Adams's face as he tapped his spurs into the sides of his horse and proceeded on down the high ridge.

'Sometimes you gotta fight fire with something a tad more powerful than water, boys.' Adams gripped his reins and led his men towards the distant lights of the town.

Tomahawk shook his head and muttered under his breath as he allowed his black gelding to follow the chestnut. 'Dynamite's a tad more powerful than water OK, Gene. That's for sure.'

EIGHT

Businessman Matt Francis stood on the balcony of his home and studied the town before him, bathed in the light of a hundred coal-oil lamps. Almost every window cast light out into the wide streets as business went on as usual. Just as on every night that had gone before, the town of Red River was alive with cowboys determined to have a good time, even if it killed them.

Cowboys from every cattle-spread on the range.

Francis knew that nearly every cent of their money would end up eventually in his deep pockets, yet he found no satisfaction in the knowledge this night.

He lifted the glass tumbler of whiskey off the wooden balustrade and swallowed the amber liquor in one go. The first swig of the day had burned his throat, but that had been fourteen hours earlier. Now he could hardly taste it. He wondered how many more glasses it would take to stop the fear from soaking his expensive shirts with sweat.

He knew it was fear that he tasted in his mouth. Pure undiluted fear. He had dark thoughts haunting him that seemed impossible to exorcise. Troublesome thoughts, that burned at his guts like a ravenous cancer.

Sucking on the end of a long thin cigar, Francis tried vainly to allow the flavour of the expensive leaf to satisfy his cravings and settle his nerves.

It could not.

There seemed to be no taste in the smoke as it filled his lungs and drifted through his teeth. For fear can affect different men in different ways and Matt Francis was afraid.

He knew there was good reason to be wary.

Since he had first sent for Billy Bob Smith and the rest of the Red River Raiders, Francis had known that it was easy to hire vermin like that, but could prove a damn sight harder to control them once they had tasted power.

Matt Francis had spent a year convincing Hooper and McCall that if they wanted the Bar 10 and the prosperity that went with it, they had to hire men who would do anything for money. Men who had no morals whatsoever.

Matt Francis had done his job well and both McCall and Hooper seemed eager for the hired killers to arrive and begin their work. Only Francis now wondered as to the sanity of his actions in sending for the Red River Raiders.

Would they stop when they had achieved their goal? Would they be satisfied with the agreed fee once they discovered the value of the Bar 10?

Would they listen to him?

As each day had passed and their inevitable arrival drew ever closer, Francis began to wonder how on earth he and his two partners could control such a gang.

The answer had come to him earlier that week.

They couldn't.

For these were not ordinary men he had sent for. These were ruthless killers. Men who, it was said, drank the blood of their victims.

Matt Francis strode to the very end of the long balcony and stared at the faraway ridge for the thousandth time. Resting his hands upon the weathered rail he gazed at a sight he could not understand. Under the blackness of a sky devoid of a moon, he noticed something strange to the east.

Something different.

Something which ought not to be there, yet was.

The sky above the rocky ridge which marked the boundary to the Bar 10 seemed to be glowing an eerie red colour. The entire rockface was in silhouette. For a brief moment the businessman just shrugged and decided that the sunset was lingering just a little longer than usual.

As Francis walked along the balcony and back into his bedroom, making his way toward the lantern-lit landing, he began to think harder about the strange sight which he had just witnessed. But when you had taken to drinking at least one bottle of whiskey a day to calm your ragged nerves, logical thought did not come easy.

If he had just been a little more sober he would have realized exactly what was troubling him about the glowing scarlet sky over in the direction of the Bar 10.

He would have remembered that the sun always sets in the west and never the east. He might even have realized that only a great fire could have illuminated the night sky that way.

But Matt Francis had not been totally sober since he had sent for the Red River Raiders.

He had good reason not to be.

NINE

Darkness covered the seemingly endless range like a protective blanket. It shielded everything except those who happened to be caught in the lights of the small town as they stretched out over the almost level land and flowing river. It was fortunate for the five Bar 10 riders that there was no moon in the black star-filled sky.

Gene Adams had led the weary cowboys for several hours across the soft lush ground toward the brightly illuminated Red River when his keen eyesight spotted the dozen riders a half mile off to their right.

The rancher dragged his chestnut mare to a halt and raised his left hand to signal his men to do the same. As usual, the faithful rannies obeyed the big man.

Tomahawk steered his black horse to the side of his oldest friend and looked up at the face bathed in shadow. It had taken hours for their tired eyes to adjust to the blackness of this strange terrain yet only Adams seemed capable of actually seeing properly.

'What's wrong, Gene?' Tomahawk whispered to the rancher whilst he too gazed out across the range, trying to spot whatever it was that had caught Adams's attention.

Adams pointed a gloved finger in the direction of the line of riders to the north. Riders who were slowly and silently approaching Red River.

'Who do you reckon they are, boys?' Adams asked his men.

Tomahawk shook his head. 'My eyes ain't good enough to make them out. Can any of you make out them riders?'

Johnny Puma moved his pinto alongside the rancher.

'They could be cowboys. I done seen a lot of cowboys riding from one place to another since we started across this range.'

'Nope. Whatever they are, they ain't cowboys, Johnny,' Adams corrected bluntly.

'I can't even make out how many there are, let alone what they are, Gene,' Happy admitted honestly.

'I count ten.' Rip nodded.

'There are twelve of them,' Adams corrected again.

'How come you reckon they ain't cowboys, Gene?' Johnny asked the rancher.

'You ever seen cowboys with that much artillery weighing their horses down, son?' Adams picked his canteen up from where it hung on the saddle horn and slowly unscrewed its stopper.

Johnny studied the riders again. With only the light of the town making it possible to see them at all, it was not easy.

'The horses do look a little low in the mud, I guess.'

'I can see rifle butts sticking out from beneath every saddle, Johnny,' Adams said. He poured water into his dry mouth and allowed it to trickle slowly down his throat. 'Cowboys don't carry rifles like that. Not unless they're looking for trouble.'

'You sure got better eyesight than me, Gene,' Johnny admitted.

'Maybe they are cowboys looking to cause a ruckus.' Tomahawk lifted his hatchet from his belt and ran his thumb along its honed edge.

'They ain't cowboys,' Adams repeated. 'That bunch are hired guns or maybe an outlaw gang looking for someplace safe to hide out.'

'Red River ain't got no law,' Happy said.

'Exactly.' Adams nodded.

'We don't wanna get tangled up with them critters, Gene.' Rip rubbed the dust from his face.

'Right!' Adams handed the canteen to the other men to share. Then he stood in his stirrups and surveyed the area carefully.

'If'n we can see them, they can see us,' Tomahawk said, slipping his axe back into his belt.

'They can't see us, old-timer,' Gene Adams drawled confidently. 'The light of the town is splashing mainly north and south but there ain't hardly no light at all coming in our direction.'

'Yeah, you're right,' Tomahawk agreed.

Happy gave a huge sigh of relief. 'I wondered why them *hombres* hadn't opened up on us by now.'

Johnny nodded his head. 'Even desperadoes don't shoot what they can't see.'

'Right! I figure them riders will take about two hours to reach Red River, the pace they're travelling at,' Adams said. 'I know we can get there in maybe half an hour if'n we spur these horses and make them run hard.'

Tomahawk ran his hand over his whiskers.

'Why would we wanna rush into Red River, Gene?'

'To get there before that bunch does.' Adams accepted his canteen back and took another swallow of its water before returning the stopper to its neck.

Johnny edged his pony even closer to the rancher.

'I know what Tomahawk is getting at, Gene. Why would we want to get to Red River any faster than normal? For all we know, them varmints will shoot us off our horses as soon as they know who we are.'

'That's right, Gene,' Happy added. 'You said them folks don't cotton to Bar 10 people.'

'They'll cotton to the hard cash I'm gonna pay them for every stick of dynamite they have, boys.' Adams patted his saddle-bags hard. The sound of coins filled each man's ears.

Rip lowered his chin on to his chest. 'I don't wanna get shot, Gene. Of all the things I ever wanted to do in my life, getting shot is the last one on the list.'

Adams nodded and hung the canteen back on his

saddle horn. 'Who said we're from the Bar 10?'

'But we are,' Rip Calloway said innocently.

'They don't know that, do they?' Adams leaned back in his saddle and sighed. 'We'll just be five cowboys visiting the town of Red River.'

The four riders suddenly realized what he meant.

'We're gonna hoodwink them critters, huh?' an excited Tomahawk asked.

'Yep.' Adams smiled. 'If anyone asks where we're from, you just say we're from the south. From San Remo.'

The five riders of the Bar 10 spurred their mounts and galloped hard through the blackness for the distant town of Red River.

TEN

Jake Hooper and Kevin McCall stared at each other across the green baize of the round gaming-table and held their cards close to their chests. This was unlike any other poker-game that went on within the walls of the busy Diamond Pin gambling hall. This one was a nightly ritual between two of the richest men in Red River. Sometimes they allowed Matt Francis to sit in, but never anyone else.

Staring at the three queens and two kings in his left hand, Kevin McCall smiled. He had never been able to master the art of the 'poker-face' but knew it did not really matter in this game. This was a private battle of wits between the town's richest men and did not amount to anything more than a temporary exchange of funds.

Hooper pushed another pile of chips into the centre of the table, which was already awash with gambling tokens.

'I'll see you, McCall.'

'Can you beat a full house? Queens over kings?'

McCall asked placing the five cards face up on the table before him.

There was a long pause before Jake Hooper discarded his hand on top of the chips.

'That's another thousand I owe you.'

Before McCall could drag his winnings to his chest he spotted the figure of Matt Francis staggering in through the open doorway of the gaming-house.

'Matt looks as if he's been hitting the bottle even harder than usual, Jake.' McCall pointed a finger at their associate. 'He's been making me a mite nervous lately.'

Hopper turned in his chair and stared across the busy gambling-hall at the man who was staggering towards them. He could not understand the dramatic change in the appearance of Francis over the last week.

'He's drunk again.'

'What the hell is wrong with him lately?' McCall asked as his fingers stacked the chips in neat coloured piles.

'Damned if I know.'

Francis stopped beside the round table and hovered as if he were about to collapse.

'Thought I'd find you dudes here,' Francis said, dragging a hard-back chair away from the table and sitting down. 'Why do you boys bother gambling? There ain't no point in it. Neither of you ever wins enough to hurt the other.'

'We like it, Matt,' McCall replied.

'But it's totally pointless.'

Hooper pulled his silver cigar-case from inside his hand-tailored coat and opened its top. He withdrew a long Havana, bit off its tip, then placed it in the corner of his mouth.

'You're drunk again, Matt. How come?'

'I ain't drunk,' Francis shouted, slamming a fist down on top of the green baize. A score of colourful chips went flying in all directions.

Hooper ran a match along the side of his silver cigar-case and held the flame to the tip of the Havana. He sucked in the strong smoke and said nothing.

'You ain't been sober in more than a week, Matt,' McCall growled at the red-faced banker. 'How come? Has something made you scared? Maybe there's something you ain't told us.'

Matt Francis aimed his attention at the narrow-eyed brothel-owner. There was a look in the eyes which made the roof of his mouth go suddenly dry.

'I've had a few whiskeys, that's all,' Francis reluctantly admitted. 'I ain't drunk. Wish I was.'

'I've known you for years, Matt,' Hooper started. 'I never seen you the worse for wear until you sent for Billy Bob Smith and his gang. Is there something eating at you that you ain't told us about?'

Francis raised a hand and signalled to one of the bargirls to bring him a drink. Then he looked at Hooper.

'It suddenly dawned on me that once the Red River Raiders get here, we ain't got no way of controlling the bastards.' Francis sighed.

The bargirl arrived at the table with a tray and rested it on the table. Francis licked his lips and stared at the whiskey bottle and three glasses. He reached for the bottle but suddenly felt the firm grip of McCall holding his forearm in check.

'You ain't having another drink until you explain exactly what you mean, Matt.'

Francis swallowed hard and glanced at the hard-faced man.

'Ain't you two half-wits figured it out?'

'Figured what out?'

Francis shook his head. 'The Red River Raiders ain't no lily-livered bunch of cowpokes, boys. These men are ruthless hard-boiled killers, the like of which we ain't ever done business with before. I suddenly realized that we've invited this scum right into the heart of our town. What if they decide that they want everything it's taken us years to accumulate? How can we stop them from killing us as well as Gene Adams and his men?'

Jake Hooper lifted the whiskey bottle and poured three glasses of whiskey.

'He's right, McCall.'

McCall picked up one of the glasses and tossed the drink down his throat in one easy action. Then he poured himself another.

'We need insurance that don't happen.'

'You figuring on hiring a gang of killers to take care of the gang of killers we already hired, McCall?' Francis asked, lifting a glass off the wet tray.

'What kinda Pandora's Box have we opened up

here, Matt?' McCall watched Francis shrug.

'This was all your idea, Matt,' Hooper said angrily. 'For more than a year now you've been telling us to send for this damn gang so we can wipe out Gene Adams and get his Bar 10 ranch for ourselves. Now you suddenly reckon that Smith might turn on us as well?'

Francis swallowed his whiskey.

'I think it still might work.'

'Then how come you're so scared?'

'I'm scared 'coz I know Smith and how he thinks sometimes,' Francis admitted.

'I thought you knew Smith and his gang personally?' McCall growled again.

'I do but we ain't bosom buddies or the like.'

Hooper charged his glass again. 'You saying he's not trustworthy? We've invited a fox into our henhouse and we just might end up the chickens in this damn deal?'

'Yep. That's why I'm scared.' For the first time since he had entered the Diamond Pin gambling hall, Francis sounded the most sober of the three businessmen.

Suddenly the sound of gunfire echoed off the wooden walls of the Diamond Pin gambling hall. Everyone rose to their feet and rushed towards the doorway. Francis, Hooper and McCall stood and moved to the window near their table and stared through the greasy glass out into the street.

'Is that them?' Hooper frantically asked Francis.

McCall pointed at the riders across the wide street.

'Yeah, is that the Red River Raiders, Matt?'

Matt Francis said nothing. He just stood open-mouthed as sweat traced down his face.

ELEVEN

A grim-faced Gene Adams held his exhausted chest-nut mare in check with one hand and aimed one of his gold-plated Colt .45's in the other. The rest of the Bar 10 riders gathered silently around their boss with their own weapons drawn on the angry drunken cowboys before them. Adams had expected some sort of reaction to their unexpected arrival in Red River, but the crowd of intoxicated cowboys brandishing their seldom-used guns made him uneasy.

'You boys had better holster them irons before me and my pals kill the lot of you.' Adams snarled down at the drunken gathering before them. It was a bluff he hoped he would not be forced to execute.

'We don't cotton to strangers in Red River, old man,' one of the cowboys shouted up at the rancher.

A younger cowboy fired twice into the night sky and howled with drunken joy. It was obvious to the riders that he had never been in a real fight before and had no idea of the possible consequences.

'Let's have us some fun with this bunch of saddle tramps, boys,' he screamed to the other gun-toting cowboys behind him. The cowboys were already holstering their weapons as they realized the danger that faced them.

Adams wrapped the reins around his saddle horn, then drew his other gun and pulled back its hammer until it fully locked.

'I don't cotton to sniffling wet-behind-the-ears children shooting at me and my friends, son.'

'There are more of us than there are of you,' the cowboy piped up again, seemingly unaware that he was now alone, his drinking friends having abandoned him to the relative safety of the gambling-hall boardwalk.

'Maybe so, but you'll be the first one to die if you shoot at us again.' Gene Adams stared hard at the youth. He had faced down many real gunmen in his day and knew exactly how to frighten mere cowboys. 'Holster that gun, little boy. We've had a long hard ride and we ain't in the best of moods.'

The cowboy, who was obviously still in his teens, spat at the ground without realizing he was now the only Red River cowboy still holding his pistol in defiance of the rancher.

'I don't like being called a little boy.'

'And I don't like being called an old man,' Adams responded.

The four other Bar 10 riders shifted their mounts to flank the steely-eyed rancher. Each of them trained their guns on the young liquor-sodden youth whilst watching the group of less reckless cowboys behind him.

'You don't scare me, old man,' the cowboy said. This time his voice had less conviction in it as he noticed his friends had deserted him.

'Takes brains to be scared, young 'un,' Tomahawk said, waving his pistol over the head of his black quarter horse. 'You strikes me as being the dumbest critter this side of the Rio Grande.'

'You got a big mouth, old-timer,' the youngster shouted at Tomahawk.

Adams leaned back in his saddle. 'It just looks big 'coz it ain't got many teeth in it, sonny. But even Tomahawk could outshoot you and he's the worst shot I've ever known.'

'Have you got any brains under that hat?' Johnny Puma moved his pinto pony slightly ahead of the line of Bar 10 men and faced down the sweating youth.

The young cowboy swiftly raised his Remington. 'I'll kill all of you bastards!'

Faster than any of the gathered crowd had ever seen anyone handle a gun before, Johnny Puma fanned the hammer of his Colt twice. The first shot took the Remington out of the kid's hand and the second tore the holster clean off the gunbelt.

There was a silence in the street after the deafening noise of gunshots faded away. When the gunsmoke finally drifted from the barrel of Johnny's gun the youngster was kneeling on the ground nursing his bleeding hand. There was disbelief carved into his features.

Johnny stared down at the young cowboy. 'I could have parted your head straight down the middle like a ripe watermelon, kid. If'n I'd wanted to.'

Adams slid one of his guns into its holster, dismounted and walked his horse towards a water trough. He signalled to his men to do the same. They did.

Matt Francis led Hooper and McCall out of the brilliantly illuminated gambling-house into the street. He had been expecting to see Billy Bob Smith and was taken aback by the sight before him. He did not recognize any of these men holding their guns in their hands.

'Who are you, stranger?' Francis asked Adams after he had pushed his way through the crowd.

Gene Adams looped his reins over a hitching rail and stared at the three men who were closing in on him. He recognized Jake Hooper from the last time he had been to Red River and prayed that a quarter of a century had blurred the memory of his rotund figure.

'Name's Smith,' Adams lied, keeping his head down so that his wide-brimmed Stetson would disguise his distinctive features.

Francis beamed.

'You must be one of Billy Bob Smith's brothers.'

Adams glanced at his men and cleared his throat before returning his attention to Francis.

'Yep. I'm one of Billy Bob's brothers. And you are?'

'Matt Francis. I sent for you boys.'

Adams nodded. 'Nice to meet you, Matt.'

'Where are the rest of the Red River Raiders?' Francis asked the rancher.

'They're a few miles back along the trail,' Adams replied, as he recalled the line of horsemen they had spotted a half-hour earlier. 'Billy Bob sent us ahead to kinda check things out. He don't like entering a town unless we've made sure it's OK.'

'When do you reckon the rest of the gang will be here?' Matt Francis asked.

'A couple of hours,' Adams said slowly, thinking about the words that had dripped from Francis's lips. The Red River Raiders were known throughout Texas. Why was this man expecting them?

'I'm sorry about the reception party, Smith,' McCall said as he closed in on the wide-shouldered rancher.

'We were expecting a lot worse,' Adams said truthfully. 'That's the trouble for us Red River Raiders, everybody likes to take a shot at us.'

'I can swear that it won't happen again, Smith,' Francis said, placing his right hand over his chest.

'What exactly is the job we're here to do? Billy Bob don't tell us nothing,' Adams drawled.

Francis leaned closer to Adams. 'Didn't he tell you about you boys attacking the Bar 10? I hired Billy Bob to kill Gene Adams and the rest of his wranglers.'

Gene Adams felt a cold chill envelop him.

'Billy Bob likes to surprise me and the rest of the gang. He likes to keep the details 'til later. He just told us that we've gotta get some supplies together.'

'I guess you boys want a bite to eat and some liquor,' Hooper speculated.

Adams turned his back on Hooper and placed a hand on the shoulder of Matt Francis.

'We want dynamite. As much as you can get together.'

Francis placed a finger at his lips and thought.

'Dynamite, huh?'

'As much as you can get together.'

'No problem. I'll make sure you'll get every stick in Red River.' Francis turned to McCall and whispered to the man.

Adams watched McCall taking a few men with him along the boardwalk in the direction of the hardware store.

'We'll have to head out before Billy Bob and the rest of the boys get here.'

Francis nodded. 'I understand,' he said knowingly.

'What about that grub and whiskey, Smith?' Hooper asked again.

Adams glanced at the rest of his Bar 10 riders who had not spoken since their boss had been cornered by Francis and his associates.

'A few whiskeys would clear the dust from our throats,' he answered.

Reluctantly, Gene Adams followed Francis and Hooper into the Diamond Pin gambling hall with his four men on his heels. With every step, the rancher wondered whether Jake Hooper's memory might return once he got a good look at the face he had last seen twenty-five years earlier. Adams decided to keep his hat on to hide his distinctive white hair.

Just in case.

TWELVE

The lush fertile ground was almost level next to the wide fast-flowing water. Only the river itself was at a lower level as it carved its way across the immense range. Occasional well-nourished trees marked out the river's route through the land that had once offered refuge to the vast herds of nomadic buffalo. Now only cattle roamed this range, totally unaware of the nobility it had replaced.

Even with no moon to guide them, the Red River Raiders had found it an easy trail to follow. All they had to do was head south along the banks of the waterway until they reached the town perched on its banks.

A thousand stars had cast their eerie light across the distinctive brows of countless white-faced cattle and off the impressive horns of their longhorn cousins during the last two days of riding.

The twelve riders knew that they were now close to the heart of the great range, which meant they would soon reach their goal.

It was a tired and sore Billy Bob Smith who stood on

the banks of the Red River and stared at the distant town from where he had just heard the sound of gunfire. Most men would have been wary upon hearing guns being fired in a town they were approaching, but not the elder Smith brother. He had been too long in the business of stealing and killing for mere gunshots to trouble him. He had reached a time in his career when having people shooting at him seemed nothing more than a normal day's occurrence.

For Smith it was an occupational hazard.

The lights of the town danced across the surface of the fast-flowing water as their horses drank their fill and his men nervously gathered around him.

Billy Bob Smith was hungry and thirsty for something stronger than the water he had been forced to drink for the last few days. The town beckoned to him. He could smell the aroma of food being cooked, drifting on the night air.

Tearing off the end of his cigar with his ragged teeth, Billy Bob shook his head and struck a match across his leather chaps.

'You hear that, Billy Bob?' Mason Pyle asked, spitting a huge lump of black goo at the ground. 'Did you hear them damn shots?'

'I ain't deaf, Pyle,' the gang leader answered cupping the flame in his gloved hands and lighting his smoke.

'Could be trouble,' the gigantic Broncho Bates said as he filled his canteen.

'Might just be a couple of high-spirited youngsters letting off a little steam,' Waco suggested.

Smoke drifted from the mouth of Billy Bob Smith. He chewed the cigar as if it were a liquorice-stick.

'Whatever it was, it's over.'

Silas Jackson managed to tear himself away from the side of Tom Hetty for a few moments. He squared up to Smith.

'How do we know that this ain't just a trap, Billy Bob? For all we know we're riding into an ambush. We got a lot of money on our heads and there's always someone ready to risk their necks for a slice of our bounty.'

'I know Matt Francis, Silas,' Smith said, picking tobacco from his teeth. 'He ain't got the guts to cross me. In fact, he's probably a bigger crook than we are. But he uses his brains to get what he wants, rather than his guns.'

Jackson returned to the side of Hetty.

The three other Smith brothers tended to their horses and also the one belonging to Billy Bob. They did not offer any thoughts on the matter. They just did as they were told the way they had always done. Each of them a deadly marksman in his own right, they had never been known to question or stand up to their older brother. He did the thinking and they just obeyed orders.

One-eyed Thaddeus Nelson kicked at the ground. He was in his usual bad mood.

'I'm hungry, Billy Bob. Why don't we make us a big fire and fry some bacon?' he suggested.

Billy Bob Smith spat out the tobacco-leaves from his mouth and wiped his tongue along his jacket-sleeve. He then nodded to the strange Nelson.

'How long do you figure it'll take to get a fire hot enough for us to cook anything, Thaddeus?' Smith asked.

'How should I know? An hour?' Nelson growled.

'And how long do you think it'll take us to reach that town over yonder?' Billy Bob pointed his smouldering cigar at the twinkling lights of Red River.

'Maybe an hour.' Nelson angrily kicked at the ground again. 'Exactly,' Billy Bob Smith said. 'By the time it takes us to get some bacon half-cooked, we can be there letting someone fry us up some inch-thick steaks.'

'But I'm still hungry!' Nelson snarled.

'You and me both.' Smith sighed.

'I still don't like the idea of us taking on the Bar 10 ranch, Billy Bob,' Tom Hetty said from the bank of the river. 'No matter how much they're willing to pay us, I still think it's suicidal to even try.'

'Why?' Smith glanced at the outlaw, who was standing shoulder to shoulder with Jackson as usual.

'I heard tell that Gene Adams has more than a hundred men protecting that spread,' Hetty replied.

Billy Bob nodded.

'I heard that as well. But they're cowpunchers not gunmen. I ain't never been scared of cowboys.'

'But they say that Adams was once a gunfighter?' Hetty added.

'A couple of hundred years ago.' Porter Bruce laughed out loud.

'Seriously though, are we gonna go up against a

hundred men?' Elmer Bruce spat at the ground.

'Maybe.' Billy Bob Smith grinned as he placed the cigar back in his mouth. 'And then again, maybe not.'

'I don't get it,' Bates said. He hung his canteen on his saddle horn.

'Matt Francis and the rest of them rich bastards in Red River must have plenty of money stashed away someplace,' Billy Bob said through a cloud of smoke. 'I figure we might just take that instead of risking our necks on the Bar 10. After all, them dudes ain't likely to stop us. Then we can head north again.'

Thaddeus Nelson almost smiled.

'Can we get us some damn grub in Red River before we steal the fillings out of their teeth, Billy Bob?'

The outlaws laughed. Gathering up their reins, one by one they mounted their horses and started out on the final leg for Red River.

This time there was more urgency in their riding. Now they were driving their horses hard. They had the scent of the town in their nostrils.

THIRTEEN

Gene Adams watched through the large window of the café as Johnny, Rip and Happy helped Matt Francis's men strap the last of the bags of dynamite on to their horses. It had taken far longer than the rancher had hoped to collect all the dynamite sticks in Red River, and Adams kept thinking about the approaching riders whom he and his pals had spotted earlier.

Tomahawk was sitting knowingly at the end of the table trying to avert the unwanted attention of the suspicious Jake Hooper from Adams. It was no easy task for the old cowboy because the businessman was becoming more and more interested in the rancher.

'You got many girls in this town, Hooper?' Tomahawk asked with a glint in his eye.

'I run the girls.' McCall cut him short.

'I'm sure that we must have met at some time, Smith,' Hooper said to Adams. 'You ever been to Red River before?'

'Maybe we have met. I've been around an awful

long time,' Adams replied, keeping his chin tucked on to his chest.

'Are the girls pretty, Hoop?' Tomahawk poked Hooper with a long bony finger.

'They were,' Hooper answered.

'They still are,' McCall protested.

'They got teeth?' Tomahawk poked his finger into the arm of Jake Hooper again.

'Some of them still have teeth.' Hooper sighed.

'Shame, I like my females gummy, like me.' Tomahawk winked at Adams who was getting uneasy at the attention Hooper was giving him.

Sweat ran down from beneath the hatband of Adams's black ten-gallon hat and dripped continuously on his shirt.

He was afraid.

Yet this was a different kind of fear. He knew that the lives of his four companions were at risk if Jake Hooper were to recognize him. Tomahawk finished his coffee and glanced briefly at Adams before moving away from the table and ambling out into the street.

Adams nodded to the old-timer through the window. It was time to get out of Red River and they both knew it.

As long as Francis and his cronies believed that Adams was one of the notorious Smith brothers, they were all safe. But he knew it was only a matter of time before Hooper recalled exactly when he had last encountered the rancher.

'Reckon the boys are ready to head out. I'll be

going now, gents,' Adams said. He pushed his half-eaten dinner away from him and dropped the napkin on top of the plate.

'How come you need all that dynamite, Smith?' McCall asked Adams curiously.

'We've got our orders from good old Billy Bob,' Adams replied. He got to his feet and waited for the other men to allow him to move away from the table.

'How do you know that you need dynamite at all? I thought you said that you didn't know what Billy Bob was planning or anything about the job he was paid to come here for?' Jake Hooper said. He looked up from his chair and looked directly at Gene Adams. For the first time he managed to get a good view of Adams's features. His expression changed. 'We have met before, Smith. I'm certain of it.'

Adams forced his way from the window table and headed for the door and the street.

'Billy Bob told me a few things. I got to rig up some surprises for that Adams critter,' Adams said over his shoulder as he walked.

The three men stood and hurriedly followed Adams out into the street. Jake Hooper rushed ahead of Francis and McCall and grabbed the sleeve of the rancher.

'Look at me, damn you. Have we ever met before? Why are you hiding your face?'

'You don't know me, Hooper,' Adams said without turning to face his inquisitor.

Hooper saw the distinctive pair of Colts in the

rancher's holsters and mumbled under his breath: 'Only one man has golden guns. I knew I recognized you. You're Gene Adams!'

Adams turned on his heels and swiftly hit the round stomach of Hooper with a short left punch. Hooper gasped as the wind was knocked out of him. As his head came forward, the rancher smashed a powerful uppercut to the jaw. The sound of breaking teeth filled the street.

Matt Francis and Kevin McCall gasped in shocked amazement when they saw Hooper staggering back from the blistering punches of Adams.

Gene Adams grabbed the thinning hair of the overweight man with his left hand and steadied him. Then he threw the hardest punch he could muster into the centre of Hooper's already bleeding face.

Hooper's feet lifted off the ground and he went flying backwards through the window of the café. Glass shattered in all directions as the limp body tumbled into the building. Gene Adams watched as Hooper's unconscious frame landed on the table that he and the others had only vacated a few minutes earlier. The table-legs snapped beneath the weight of the large man, sending him crashing on to the floor.

Johnny Puma rode his pinto pony between Adams and the stunned onlookers.

'What on earth was that all about, Smith?' Francis asked Adams from a respectable distance.

Gene Adams glanced at the two men and then turned to the Bar 10 cowboys atop their mounts. He accepted the reins to his chestnut from Johnny before replying to Francis:

'He touched me, Matt,' Adams said coldly.

Francis felt his throat growing dry.

'He touched you? Is that all?'

Adams grabbed the saddle horn, poked his left boot into the stirrup and hauled himself up on to the mare. He knew they were running out of time. The real Red River Raiders could arrive at any moment.

'I don't cotton to being touched, Matt.' Adams tipped the brim of his hat and turned his horse.

Francis and McCall watched the five riders gallop away from the café. Soon they had disappeared into the darkness of the range.

'That Smith critter is a mite edgy, Matt.'

Francis shook his head and sighed heavily. His heart was racing as he suddenly remembered something.

'I touched his shoulder when he first arrived, McCall. That could have been me lying in my own blood and not Hooper.'

McCall looked in at the mess which had once been the living Jake Hooper. He laughed.

'I've wanted to do that to him for years.'

'Yeah, he ain't never looked so good.'

Both men continued laughing and headed for the Diamond Pin.

The five horses had already ridden further and harder than they had ever done before. It was a desperate Gene Adams who led Tomahawk and the others across the grazing land at full gallop. There was no time to lose. The very existence and survival of their Bar 10 was at stake.

But that was not the only reason the riders of the Bar 10 were racing back to the cattle ranch. There was also the little problem of the Red River Raiders. Adams wanted to put as much space between the small town and himself as possible before its inhabitants discovered the truth about their recent visitors.

Adams had already learned that Francis and his cronies had hired the most lethal gang of rustlers and murderers in Texas to raid the Bar 10. As he spurred his horse on, he wondered whether they would still try to attack his ranch, knowing that Gene Adams was now aware of their plan.

It all hinged on how long it would take Jake Hooper to regain consciousness and learn to talk with fewer teeth. Once Hooper spilled the beans to Francis and McCall about whom they had given all of Red River's explosives to, things might change. Would even the Red River Raiders be foolhardy enough to attempt striking at the Bar 10 when they knew that Gene Adams had already been informed of the impending bloodbath?

But Adams had learned long ago that men did insane things when their pride was at stake. There was no logic in the actions of men who killed for a living.

This chilling thought alone kept Adams riding as he had never ridden before.

Before leaving Red River, Tomahawk had filled his

saddle-bags with hundreds of long five-minute fuses. The other four riders carried the actual sticks of explosives. They all knew you could not take risks with dynamite. Theirs was a deadly cargo which they had strapped down well.

Their valiant horses were now all snorting with exhaustion as their masters mercilessly drove them on and on. Adams knew their precious mounts deserved better treatment than they had received over the last twenty-four hours, yet he had to be ruthless. The entire Bar 10 ranch was at stake and he knew that if he failed to stop the inferno that was engulfing it soon, there would be no ranch left.

Only blackened cinders.

Even if it meant risking bursting the hearts of the horses beneath them, they had to keep forging ahead.

There was no alternative.

No other way.

They had no choice.

Thrashing his reins from one shoulder of the chestnut mare to the other with his loyal men at his side, Adams suddenly caught the aroma of burning in his nostrils. Pushing the wide brim of his hat back off his face he suddenly saw the crimson sky over the far-off ridge.

Even from this great distance, the blaze was evident. Burning cinders floated on the gentle breeze above their heads like a million fireflies.

How far had the fire spread since he and his men had ridden west, Adams wondered. Had it reached the centre of the Bar 10 already? If so, he knew his mission had been in vain. There was only one place where it might just be possible to stop the raging flames in their tracks: one spot where he could plant the dynamite sticks and have a chance of halting the fire's relentless advance. If the fire had already swept past that place, all was lost.

Spurring the horse yet again, Adams forced the chestnut to find even greater pace.

There was fevered desperation in his gloved hands as they nursed the reins in a desperate bid to make his mount reach his beloved Bar 10. The flat land slowly gave way to the slow incline which the five riders knew led up into the ridge of mountainous rock that marked the boundary to their ranch.

Somehow they had keep their spent horses moving ever upward until they reached the sanctuary of the line shack that marked the most westerly outpost of the Bar 10.

Once there, Adams knew they could exchange their lathered-up mounts for fresh ones. Then they could head down towards the heart of the ranch and try to stop the fire before it consumed everything he had spent four decades building.

But it was a long hazardous climb to reach the summit of the ridge in daylight, let alone at night.

Darkness was now another foe they had to defeat.

FOURTEEN

Matt Francis felt his ribs cave in from the hefty blow. If his arms had not been held behind his back by the huge Broncho Bates, he might have just ridden the punch. But he was being held in place by one of the strongest men in Texas. Held in check to be beaten by the smiling Billy Bob Smith.

'Stop!' Francis screamed.

Smith turned to his fellow outlaws and growled.

'I told you this place was filled with cowards, didn't I?'

Waco stepped forward and stared down at the remains of Kevin McCall.

'What the hell are you killing these insects for, Billy Bob?'

'Because they lied to me,' Smith retorted kicking Francis hard in the stomach.

'I ain't heard no lies.' Waco snorted.

Smith screwed up his eyes and stared hard at the outlaw. He did not like being contradicted and it showed.

'This critter Francis told me that my brother had

been here already and that he had given the bastard every stick of dynamite in the town. I call that lying. What do you call it?'

Waco looked at the figure of Francis, now being held upright by the powerful arms of Bates.

'He told you that some critter calling himself Smith rode in with four sidekicks. Somehow Francis ended up being conned. He also told you that this Smith bastard beat up their partner Jake Hooper before they headed off toward the Bar 10.'

Smith brooded.

'So?'

'Does that make killing the dumb idiots right?' Waco was troubled by Billy Bob Smith's actions since they had arrived in Red River. They had always been an evil bunch but to kill the men who had already paid you fifty per cent of your fee seemed too much even for the famed Raiders.

Smith stared down at the body of Matt McCall and gritted his teeth.

'I didn't mean to kill that weasel,' he admitted.

'So let's find this Jake Hooper character and get him to tell us why the man named Smith beat the daylights out of him.' Waco pulled half a cigar from his coat pocket and placed it between his teeth. 'Maybe then we'll know who is and who ain't telling us the truth.'

Billy Bob Smith signalled to Broncho Bates. The giant outlaw released his grip and allowed Matt Francis to fall to the ground.

'Come on, boys. Waco's right. Let's find this Hooper varmint.'

Thaddeus Nelson rubbed his belly. 'What the hell are you so all fired up about? Who gives a damn? Them five riders never took our money, only dynamite. Let's eat.'

Smith drew one of his guns, thrust it into Nelson's one good eye and cocked its hammer.

'If'n you don't wanna end up with no eyes, Thaddeus, I'd quit your opinionating right now. Understand?'

'OK. OK.' Nelson croaked.

It was not far from the saloon to the café. A matter of only twenty paces. The dozen outlaws had already scared away most of the unwanted witnesses when they had first arrived in town with their guns blazing into the night sky. Terrified cowboys had fled in all directions when Smith had led his dust-covered riders into the wide streets of Red River and slaughtered McCall.

The light of the flickering oil-lanterns danced over the glass splinters strewn out into the street. The fragments of glass that littered the boardwalk beneath the smashed café window were different though.

Dried blood coated them.

Jake Hooper's blood.

Billy Bob Smith stepped up on to the boardwalk and stared into the building. Jake Hooper was still lying where he had landed after being knocked senseless by Gene Adams.

'That must be the critter.' Smith pointed.

Mason Pyle, Joey Smith and Porter Bruce entered

the building, hauled Hooper's unconscious body up off the café floor and dragged it out into the street.

'This guy's a mess, Billy Bob,' Joey Smith told his elder brother.

'He's in better shape than Francis and the other dude.' Nelson laughed loudly.

'Wake him,' Smith ordered.

Elmer Bruce removed his Stetson and scooped water from the closest trough and threw it over Hooper. For a few seconds there was no reaction, then the man began to splutter.

Blood poured from Hooper's mouth when he coughed. The bruised eyes opened and rolled in his head before he managed to focus on the men standing before his propped-up body.

'You Jake Hooper?' Smith asked, kicking the shoe of the bewildered man.

Somehow Hooper nodded. A tooth fell from his mouth when he tried to reply. There was a shocked expression carved across the gambling-hall man's face which made the outlaws laugh.

'Somebody sure made a mess of you, *amigo*,' Smith remarked. 'The question is, who?'

'It . . . it was Gene Adams,' Hooper managed to say as even more pieces of teeth fell from his bleeding mouth.

Billy Bob Smith's expression suddenly changed. He snapped his fingers for Caleb and Kermit to pick Hooper up off the ground. As always, his brothers did exactly as they were ordered.

'Say again, old-timer.' Billy Bob Smith leaned

closer to the bloated features of Jake Hooper. 'Did you say that Gene Adams did this to you?'

'Yep. It was Adams, OK,' Hooper replied from the arms of the two Smith brothers.

Tom Hetty stepped forward and took a closer look at the battered man.

'I thought you said Adams was an old man, Billy Bob.'

'He is. He has to be by now. The critter has owned the Bar 10 since before I was born.'

'No old man could do that to anyone.' Hetty pointed at Hooper's face. 'This Adams must hit as hard as a mule kicks if'n this varmint is anything to go by.'

'It couldn't have been Adams,' Smith snapped. 'This man has had his brains mashed. He's all mixed up and turned around.' Hetty grabbed Hooper's head and tilted it back.

'Are you certain it was Adams, mister?'

'It was him OK.' Hooper sighed heavily as more blood and fragments of teeth dripped from his mouth. 'I recognized his guns.'

'What about his guns?' Hetty shook Hooper's head violently.

'They're gold. Golden guns.' Hooper managed to reply.

Hetty released his grip on Hooper's head and stood square on to Smith.

'Golden guns?'

'I heard about them guns. Hooper's right.' Smith ran his fingers over his bewhiskered features and began to shake. The other outlaws had seen their leader like this before. There was a madness which haunted the eldest Smith brother. A madness that could boil over at any moment.

'Something don't figure here, Billy Bob,' Silas Jackson said biting his lower lip.

'Yeah.' Billy Bob Smith smouldered. 'So Adams ain't like normal folks. He somehow ain't gotten old like the rest of us.'

Mason Pyle spat at the ground and wiped the spittle off his chin.

'Let's just clean this town of its money and head back north, Billy Bob.'

The eldest Smith brother walked to the edge of the boardwalk and rested an arm against the wooden upright. He pondered over the situation.

'Why would Adams risk his neck coming here? I heard tell that he's the most hated man in these parts. Why would he come here and what the hell does he want with dynamite?'

'Mason's right, Billy Bob,' Joey said, grabbing at his brother's sleeve. 'Let's take the money Francis promised us and ride back north.'

Smith looked briefly at his brother.

'Something made that Adams come to Red River to get them explosives, but what?'

Even with only one good eye, Nelson was a lot more observant than his partners. He brushed up beside Smith and pointed at the distant ridge. The glowing red sky could not now be mistaken for anything other than what it was.

'Look, Billy Bob. The Bar 10 is ablaze.'

Smith pushed the brim of his hat back off his temple and screwed his eyes up tight.

'Nelson's right. Adams's ranch is on fire, boys.'

FIFTEEN

Even though it was still the middle of the night, the blazing eastern section of the Bar 10 lit up the entire ranch as if it were bathed in daylight. But no sun ever cast such an eerie satanic light as the rampant flames did. Like a nest of gigantic red snakes the light coiled and struck out at everything within its reach. Adams and his men found themselves watching the terrifying sight far below their vantage point as they transferred their saddles and bags from their spent mounts to the fresh cutting horses.

'We ain't got a lotta time, Gene,' Tomahawk pointed out to the grim-faced rancher. 'That fire must have destroyed nearly half the pasture land on the Bar 10.'

'We ain't licked yet,' Adams insisted.

'You figure that this dynamite is the answer, Gene?' Johnny Puma asked. He pushed his pinto pony into the small corral and closed the makeshift gate.

'If it ain't, we're gonna be out of a job for quite some time, Johnny,' Gene Adams replied.

'At least until the new grass grows again.' Tomahawk coughed as the smoke of the far-off fire filled his lungs. The air tasted like charcoal in the mouths of the five men.

Gene Adams hurriedly removed his saddle from the exhausted chestnut and threw it on to the back of one of the four cutting horses stabled on the high ridge of the western outpost. Happy Summers was already stepping into the stirrup of his new mount as the troubled Rip approached the busy rancher.

'What about me, Gene?' Rip Calloway asked the rancher, who was soaked in sweat as he feverishly tightened the cinch straps of his Texan saddle.

'You have to stay here and keep a look-out for the Red River Raiders, Rip,' Adams said patting the young cowboy on his shoulder. 'We'll have our work cut out for us fighting that fire. We ain't got time to worry about them rustlers creeping up behind us.'

'But I wanna help you and the boys fight that fire,' Calloway protested.

Adams opened one of the satchels of his saddle-bags, withdrew a half-dozen sticks of dynamite and handed them to the wrangler. Rip's eyes widened when he looked at the brown sticks of explosives.

'This is how you can help the rest of the boys, Rip,' Adams said bluntly.

Rip Calloway held the sticks cautiously. He had never handled anything so deadly before and it showed in his strained expression.

'I'll probably blow myself sky-high with this stuff, Gene. I ain't never played around with this dynamite before. I'm a wrangler, not a quarry man. '

Adams placed his saddle-bags behind the cantle of his saddle and secured the leather laces firmly before moving to Tomahawk and his fresh mount.

'Give me a handful of fuses, old-timer,' Adams told his oldest friend. 'Dynamite ain't much use without fuses.'

Tomahawk pulled out six fuses and gave them to the rancher. 'You leaving Rip here with this stuff?'

Adams hesitated. 'What you mean?'

'He's likely to kill himself with these.' Tomahawk pointed his bearded chin in the direction of the pale cowboy who was visibly shaking. 'You gotta know what ya doing when you plays around with this stuff. Rip's second to none at punching steers but he ain't got no idea how to handle dynamite, Gene.'

Gene Adams's head turned. He glanced at the sweating features of the young cowboy.

'Is old Tomahawk right, Rip?'

'That's the truth, Gene,' Rip said anxiously, looking around the faces of the other Bar 10 men. 'I'm plumb scared and I ain't worried who knows it.'

'You ain't ever handled dynamite before, Rip?' Adams rested a gloved hand on the arm of the cowboy.

'No, sir. I ain't.'

'You can't leave him here to do this. He'll kill himself for sure,' Tomahawk said.

'Tomahawk's right, Gene,' Johnny added, pointing down at the inferno which awaited their arrival. 'Rip will be more help with us down there.'

Adams rubbed the back of his damp neck. 'We ain't got time for this kinda delay.'

'What's holding everything up, boys?' Happy asked as he steadied the nervous gelding.

Adams had but moments to spare in making a decision. He could see that the fire far below them in the distance was now reaching the very spot on the Bar 10 where he had to try and stop it.

'What if I leave you here to do this, Tomahawk?' Adams asked the old-timer. 'Can you handle it?'

'You can rely on me, Gene.' Tomahawk wrinkled up his eyes in a way that proved that you did not require teeth to smile. 'I can throw dynamite sticks as good as I can throw my trusty old tomahawk.'

Gene Adams grabbed the sticks of dynamite from Rip's sweating hands and handed them to the skinny old man. He tugged the beard which jutted out at him.

'You know what to do if them varmints show themselves.'

'I'll blow them coyotes into a million pieces if they even poke their noses over that ridge, Gene,' Tomahawk replied watching his four friends mounting the fresh horses. 'They'll not set foot on our Bar 10. I promise ya that.'

'In a way I kinda wish that them Red River Raiders do try and invade our land, Tomahawk,' Adams grinned. 'I'd like to see you blow them apart.'

'You get that fire snuffed out, sonny.' Tomahawk winked up at the rancher.

'And you take care of yourself, Tomahawk.'

Adams swung the cutting horse around and tossed a box of matches into the bony hands. He waved to the old man as he led Johnny, Rip and Happy down through the rocks towards the heart of the ranch.

Tomahawk watched the riders galloping away from the shack perched high on the side of the high ridge. He licked his lips before turning towards the trail that led to the highest point on the ranch. Walking slowly towards it, he wondered if he really could throw a stick of dynamite as accurately as he could wield his hatchet.

He had never failed to hit whatever he aimed his deadly axe at in the past, but was troubled that his eyes weren't as sharp as the lethal blade any longer.

But Tomahawk would try. If they came, he would try his damnedest.

SIXTEEN

Billy Bob Smith stared coldly into the faces of his eleven fellow Raiders and smiled. It was a chilling sight, even to those who knew the outlaw well.

For when Smith smiled it meant trouble.

'What you thinking about, Billy Bob?' Broncho Bates asked, looking up from the remnants of his steak dinner.

'Yeah, I don't like it when you start to grin like that, partner.' Mason Pyle agreed with his gigantic associate as they watched the eldest Smith walking around the small café kicking at the fragments of glass that still littered the floor.

Billy Bob Smith paused and stared hard at the men he had ridden with for more than a decade.

'I just thought about all the gold coin that must be stashed in Gene Adams's ranch house, boys.'

Kermit Smith felt the hair on his neck tingle. That usually meant trouble for all concerned.

'Brother Billy Bob?'

'Don't start fretting, Kerm.' Smith laughed. 'We ain't heading into no bloodbath like Matt Francis

91

wanted us to do.'

Kermit sighed. 'That's a relief, I was scared you wanted us to head on over to the Bar 10 for a moment.'

'I do!' Billy Bob Smith exclaimed.

'What?' Elmer Bruce stood up from his meal in a mixture of shock and anger.

'I don't like the idea of that Adams critter having all that dynamite, Billy Bob,' Joey said shaking his head over his dinner-plate. 'Stands to reason that he'll use it on us if we even look at his ranch.'

'Easy, son.' Smith's eyes narrowed as he looked hard on his men. 'I ain't intending us going in to have no fight. I intends us to ride into the Bar 10 and just take Gene Adams money.'

'And he'll let us have it without there being a fight?' Waco snarled angrily, pushing his plate away from him. 'Are you plain loco?'

There was a hushed silence in the café. The other Red River Raiders knew just how sensitive the eldest Smith brother was at any suggestion that he was crazy. For unknown to anyone except the Smith boys themselves, both their parents had ended their days in asylums.

'You reckon I'm ready for the madhouse, Waco?' Smith screamed at the outlaw.

Waco kicked his chair away from behind him and moved out from the table where the nine other men were seated.

'If the shoe fits, I reckon you ought to wear it, Billy Bob.'

'You calling me crazy?' Smith turned square on to face the defiant outlaw. 'Well, are ya?'

'Sounds crazy to me to go into the Bar 10 when Adams knows that we've been hired to raid his ranch, don't it?' Waco yelled back as he edged away from the table.

'I ain't loco.' Smith flexed his fingers over the guns in his holsters.

'Maybe you ain't, but it sure sounds like a loco idea to me,' Waco retorted.

'But it ain't.' Smith gritted his teeth.

'I'm cutting out,' Waco announced.

'Nobody quits the Red River Raiders without my say-so.' Smith sneered ominously.

'We've already stripped Francis's bank of every cent in its safe, Smith,' Waco said, stepping closer to the leader of the gang. 'Give me my share and I'll ride out.'

'You snivelling coward,' Smith spat. 'You think I'm gonna give you anything except lead, then it's you who's loco.'

Waco eyed the rest of the outlaws who continued eating. Then he returned his gaze to the angry Billy Bob.

'But why do you wanna go to the Bar 10 and fight Adams and his men? We got ourselves a fortune already in our saddle-bags.'

'I heard tell that Gene Adams has more gold coin in his ranch than they got in the mint,' Smith gushed greedily. 'They say that man has been hoarding golden eagles for forty or more years, Waco. Can you imagine how much money that is? A fortune that makes Matt Francis's bank money look like chicken-feed.'

'But to ride in and risk fighting him and his men?'

'Adams has a fire burning up his precious ranch, Waco. Do you think he'll have time to fight us?' Smith grinned once again. It was still the grin of a man who walked the thin line between sanity and madness. 'He'll not notice us stealing his fortune 'coz he's got bigger things to worry about.'

Waco rubbed his chin.

'Are you sure?'

Smith raised an arm and pointed out towards the ridge. The sky was bright with the fire that lay far beyond.

'Look at that sky, you yellow bastard. You ever seen so much smoke? We can ride in and out of the Bar 10 without nobody batting an eyelid.'

Waco shrugged and nodded.

'OK.'

SEVENTEEN

Gene Adams drove the cutting horse into the court-yard of his ranch and dragged the reins to his broad chest. The animal stopped as the rancher's three companions pulled up beside him. He had lived in this place for over four decades and yet it seemed different. For the first time since he had first settled this land, there were no cattle in his vast stock-pens or corrals.

All four riders sat in their saddles and stared in disbelief at the sight a mere ten miles away over the rocky bluff. Glowing embers floated high above them, dangerously seeking something new to ignite. Flames leapt more than 200 feet into the blackened sky as the fire continued its relentless march across the Bar 10 towards them.

Even at this distance the heat of the unchecked inferno was enough to make even the toughest skin aware of its presence.

Adams dismounted quickly and checked the bags

he had secured to the cantle of his saddle.

'Now what?' Rip Calloway asked the sweating rancher.

'You and Happy ride to the boys who are out there trying to fight this monster, Rip,' Adams ordered.

'And?' Happy drew his horse level with the grim older man.

'And tell them to get the hell out of there,' Adams replied bluntly.

Johnny Puma dropped off the back of his horse and held tightly on to the reins until he had time to tie them securely to the ranch house hitching pole.

'You mean that the fire has won, Gene?' Johnny asked the big man beside him.

Adams moved to Happy's horse, swiftly untied the saddle-bags and tossed them over the neck of his own mount.

'The fire ain't won, Johnny,' Adams retorted. He went to Rip's horse and removed his saddle-bags too. 'But we gotta get them boys out of there now.'

Rip watched Adams walking to Johnny's mount and laying the saddle-bags over the neck of the animal.

'But if we're pulling the boys back, surely that means the fire is beyond our ability to stop it?'

Adams shook his head. He filled his dry canteen from the almost empty trough.

'It means I don't want any of my boys within spitting distance of the front of that fire when I set this dynamite off.'

Happy moved his mount closer to the rancher.

'When we round up the boys, should we bring them straight back here?'

Adams stared up into the usually jovial face. A face that was grim with fear.

'Nope. Not straight back here, Happy. Whatever you do, don't come back through the pass. I don't want you boys riding into danger. Take them up to the northern pastures and down along the Smoky River. That'll keep you all out of danger until after the job's done.'

'That's a good half-day's ride, Gene,' Happy said.

'I know that, son.' Adams nodded.

'But the Smoky River leads back here,' Rip questioned. 'Or at least to within half a mile of here, Gene.'

'A half-mile west of here, Rip,' Adams corrected. 'That's half a mile which could save all of your lives if my plan don't pan out the way I figure.'

'So me and Rip have just gotta shepherd the boys to safety?' Happy asked. 'Is that all?'

'That's the most important job of all, Happy. I'm relying on you two to lead the rest of the boys to safety.' Adams pointed a gloved finger up at the rotund wrangler. 'By now they'll be half dead and blinded from that damn fire. They need two fresh men to guide them out of there. OK?'

Happy seemed reassured by the words of the rancher. He and Rip turned their horses and thundered out of the Bar 10 courtyard and headed east towards the fire.

Johnny stepped next to Adams, who was watching the dust of the two cowboys.

'So it's just you and me, Gene.'

'Just like the good old days, Johnny.' Adams forced a smile, stepped into his stirrup and hauled his weary body back on to the cutting horse.

The young cowboy grabbed his saddle horn with both hands and threw himself on to the back of his mount. Grappling with the reins, he steered the nervous horse next to Gene.

'Apart from blowing something up, what exactly is this plan of yours, Gene?' Johnny asked the straight-backed horseman.

Gene Adams glanced at Johnny for a few seconds. Then he raised a hand and pointed in the direction where Rip and Happy had just disappeared on their mission to locate the rest of his ranch hands. Even in the middle of a seemingly endless night with the shimmering light of the raging fire swirling over the ranch, the distant rocky bluff could be easily spotted.

'The bluff?' Johnny Puma muttered.

'Yep. The bluff.'

'What about it?'

'That bluff is a wall of solid rock, maybe forty-foot high, which stretches for about ten miles in either direction, son,' Adams drawled. 'It's the only thing left between us and those flames. We drive the cattle through the pass from one place to another without even noticing it's there. But it is there and I figure if we blow up both sides of its rockface, we can create a natural barrier to stop that fire. If we don't, the fire will just funnel through the pass and burn up what's left of the Bar 10.'

Johnny stared hard at the man who was like a father to him. 'You sure it'll work?'

Adams sighed. 'Nope. That's why I wanted the boys well away from the pass before the fireworks start.'

'Will a barrier put the fire out?'

'It'll stop it reaching the rest of the ranch, Johnny.' Adams shrugged, wrapping his reins around his gloved hands. 'Everything east of the bluff is gone.'

'It'll grow back,' Johnny reassured the rancher.

'Yep.' Adams smiled. 'It'll grow back.'

Both riders tapped their spurs into the sides of their horses and started off for the bluff. By the time they had ridden past the corrals they were at full gallop.

There was no time to lose.

EIGHTEEN

Like a dozen mounted phantoms, the dust-caked Red River Raiders spurred their horses on towards the Bar 10. For more than two hours they had headed straight towards the high ridge which was silhouetted against the glowing red sky beyond. Their steady pace had not altered since they had left the ransacked town of Red River. These were men who knew their business well and how to execute it and cope with anything else that got in their way. Once primed for action, nothing could divert them from their chosen goal.

Each deadly rider had his saddle-bag filled to over-flowing with the wealth of the town far behind them. To most this would have been enough to have made their long hard ride south to Red River worthwhile in itself.

But these men wanted more.

Billy Bob Smith had managed to convince his followers that there was an even bigger prize waiting for them just over the high rocky ridge.

The Bar 10!

At any other time even the thought of being so foolhardy as to try and strike out at Gene Adams's cattle empire would have been deemed suicidal, but this was not the familiar Bar 10 ranch that awaited their ominous arrival. The billowing smoke and glowing heavens bore witness to that.

The land that lay over the high ridge was like an injured animal licking its wounds.

This was not the real Bar 10.

This was a mere shadow of the famed cattle spread. Even from the distant town of Red River it had been obvious that the Bar 10 was in trouble.

A fire that equalled anything in the mythic Hades was sending its satanic light into the night sky and filling their nostrils with the acrid scent of burnt offerings.

If ever there was a time when the Bar 10 could be taken, it was now.

Billy Bob Smith had been fast to realize that.

Every one of the twelve riders knew this chance might never come their way again.

They had to strike whilst Gene Adams's back was turned, whilst he and his cowboys were desperately trying to save what was left of the cattle empire before it turned entirely into ashes. Smith and his men knew that if they went in with their guns blazing, and the element of surprise on their side, they might even take control of the ranch for good.

The Bar 10 could be theirs!

They reached the end of the lush flat range and the riders began to navigate the incline up the rocky ridge. Thaddeus Nelson moved his mount closer to the outlaw leader.

Tapping Smith on the arm, one-eyed Nelson pointed to the highest point of the ridge a half-mile above them.

'Look, Billy Bob. I spy a man up there.'

Billy Bob Smith stood in his stirrups and stared at the figure illuminated by the light of the deadly inferno.

'I see him.'

'I wonder who that bastard is?' Waco asked aloud.

'Whoever the critter is, he'll be dead meat before sunrise, boys,' Smith vowed.

Tomahawk knew that the five-minute fuses Gene Adams had left him were far too long if he were going to blow the Red River Raiders out of their saddles, should they decide to risk attacking the Bar 10.

Using the razor-sharp blade of his trusty Indian hatchet, the old-timer cut the fuses down to size. He estimated that the three inches of fuse-wire he was forcing into the dynamite would take less than twenty seconds to burn to the explosive sticks.

It was a crude guess by anyone's yardstick but guesswork was all Tomahawk had to go by. If he had calculated the required length of fuses incorrectly, the first one would explode before he had time to throw it.

Tomahawk gave the possibility little thought.

He just remained seated in the rocks at the top of

the ridge and watched the vast plain below him for any hint of danger, as his experienced hands worked feverishly.

Every so often his old head would turn and glance back at the fire which was still raging behind him on the ranch. It was a sight he was glad his ancient eyes could not see properly.

Then Tomahawk forced himself to return his attention to the range which was still bathed in the darkness that only a moonless sky could render.

There was no detail there either.

Just a blackness that chilled his spine.

Tomahawk knew only too well that he could not see as he had once been able to see, and that bothered the wily old man. To him the flat range and the Red River that cut through it, were nothing more than a blur that he had to hope would somehow give him a clue of approaching danger.

A danger that sight alone would not anticipate.

His hearing was still as sharp as it had always been, though, and he prayed that this would serve him well should the infamous outlaw gang come within range.

If they made even the slightest of noises, he would hear it.

The snapping of a twig beneath the hoof of a stumbling horse or even a muffled cough would be enough for Tomahawk to guess the distance and rough direction any uninvited guests might choose to use.

That was all he required to send his deadly axe seeking its unseen prey, or one of the deadly sticks of dynamite in search of its target.

Just the merest hint of a sound would be enough.

Tomahawk had distant memories of his early days when he lived amongst the Indians in the vast forests of the north. Days when you could not always see your enemy but you learned how to track and kill them by using your skill as a hunter.

The Indians had raised him as one of their own and he had lived with them until he suddenly realized that he was different from those he had always considered his family.

Now all that remained of those times were his skill with his tomahawk and the ability to track any living creature across even solid ground until he caught his prey.

Tomahawk pushed the last trimmed fuse into the sixth stick of dynamite and laid them down beside him.

Were they coming?

Tomahawk knew the Bar 10 was a pretty big prize. It had tempted less able foes to try their luck before.

The old man unscrewed the stopper of his canteen and was lifting it to his lips when he heard a sound that alerted his every instinct into action.

Turning over on his belly, Tomahawk stared down into the dark shadows.

They were coming, he thought.

NINETEEN

Both men could barely believe the blistering heat that greeted their arrival at the bluff. Gene Adams and Johnny stopped their skittish mounts at the mouth of the pass which led through the unnamed rockface. The air was burning their lungs as they dismounted and led the two horses to cover beside a twisted dead tree. Adams wrapped the reins around the trunk of the tree and tied his best wrangler's knot. Neither man wanted to risk being left in this desolate place on foot should their two wide-eyed horses take flight. Holding on to his bridle, Johnny wrestled with his own terrified mount until Adams had managed to wrap the younger cowboy's reins securely around the tree.

Both men wished that they had their own trusty mounts with them instead of these seldom-used cutting horses. Yet even the most highly trained of horses would have sensed that death was already too close for comfort.

Smoke funnelled unchecked through the quarter-mile of level ground between the rocks and made seeing and breathing almost impossible. The fire was

107

now at the other side of the rocky bluff and stray embers had already ignited the few patches of dry grass scattered through the bone-dry pass.

Adams knew that with the slightest of breezes, the flames would leap that final few hundred yards and claim the rest of his ranch.

Adams untied his bandanna and made a mask for his face. With his mouth covered, he frantically worked to get the explosives readied.

Johnny Puma hauled the two saddle-bags from his horse and crouched down next to the kneeling figure of Adams who had already opened the satchels of his own pair.

'Fuses, Johnny.' Adams coughed, holding out his gloved hand to the young cowboy. 'Quickly, give me half the fuses.'

'OK!' Johnny scooped as many of the five-minute fuses from one of his bags as he could and dropped them on to the ground beside the rancher. Adams tried to insert the fuses into the necks of the dynamite sticks but his gloved hands made every move clumsy.

'Damn!' exclaimed the rancher.

For as long as any man who had ever known Gene Adams would have testified on oath, he had seldom been seen without his pair of leather gloves stretched over his large hands.

He did occasionally remove the right glove when eating or washing, but for some reason, Adams had never been seen to take the left one off.

There had been a thousand theories about

Adams's left hand over the years but nobody had ever put them to the man himself, for he was someone who guarded his secrets well.

Johnny pulled off his own gloves and started helping the older man to prime the explosives.

'Don't worry, Gene. I can get all these fuses set.'

Adams rested on his knees and gazed in horror over the shoulder of his friend. The light of the range fire was blinding and was not going to wait for anything or anyone. He had to act now.

To delay for even a few moments could be fatal.

The fire had become a living creature as it had moved half-way across the Bar 10. It had fuelled its insatiable appetite with whatever had lain in its path. It was still hungry, and Adams knew it.

'That fire ain't gonna wait, Johnny. This is a two-man, four-hand job.' Adams pulled off his right glove and pushed it into his pocket. Then to the surprise of his pal, Adams removed its matching twin from his left hand. 'C'mon, Lets get on with it, Johnny.'

Johnny stared at the left hand that Adams had always kept hidden. Its skin looked as though it had been melted by something long ago. Something which had been merciless. There were no fingernails left but the hand was fully mobile and amazingly flexible.

'Ugly, huh?' Adams asked.

'I've seen worse.'

'It was a fire, Johnny,' Adams explained, holding on to the fuses and pushing them into the sticks of dynamite at an incredible speed. 'A long, long time ago.'

Johnny nodded as he watched the hands of his friend priming the explosives at a speed that was faster than his own were capable of matching.

'Does it hurt?'

'Not any more, son,' Adams replied. 'It stopped giving me grief before you were even thought of.'

'I ain't never seen what fire can do to skin before, Gene.' The voice of the cowboy was shaking.

Gene Adams pulled his bandanna down off his face and gritted his teeth. There was a steely determination in the tanned face which Johnny had seen many times before.

'This fire ain't gonna win. I swear it.'

TWENTY

Unknown to Tomahawk, Billy Bob Smith and his men had dismounted from their horses at the foot of the ridge and fanned out before starting up the steep incline toward his hiding-place.

These were men who had outwitted all attempts by the law to catch them for more than a decade. They knew that to approach the one man they had spotted up on the top of the ridge could be done in two different ways. They could file up in a long line and give him the opportunity to cut them down at will, or they could spread themselves as wide as possible leaving a much more difficult target. The latter option would also allow them to pin their prey down in a crossfire once they got within range of the summit.

Billy Bob Smith was probably one of the worst men in Texas but knew his business well.

Their guns and rifles were cocked and readied for use.

If Tomahawk had been able to see them, he would have witnessed a wall of heavily armed men heading straight towards him. The Red River Raiders intended to use their arsenal as soon as they got the shadowy figure within their sights.

The ancient eyes of Tomahawk stared down the rocky slope into the blackness. In a way he was fortunate that he could not see the spine-chilling vision that was closing in on him. It was a sight that would have scared most grown men.

He might not have caught sight of them yet but his keen hearing had detected something heading up towards him, although, hard as he tried, he could not actually make them out.

But he knew they were there and getting closer with every passing moment.

It had been more than ten minutes since Tomahawk had first heard the unmistakable sound of Winchester repeating rifles being cocked out in the gloom below him. Ten minutes that felt like a lifetime. But Tomahawk knew that even though some men might be able to walk as silently as mountain lions when they wanted to, their shod horses could not.

Tomahawk could hear the disgruntled snorts of the animals being led up behind the approaching gunmen.

Sweat rolled down from beneath Tomahawk's battered hat and trailed along his unkempt hair until it fell on the buckskin sleeve of his jacket.

Tomahawk moved back behind a large boulder, struck a match and lit the lengths of discarded fuses. It began to burn angrily in the bony old hand. Then the cantankerous old cowboy used this fuse to light another of the spare fuses. It too began to spit out its sparks over the rocky ground.

Tomahawk placed one of the burning fuses on the ground and crawled a few feet back to the top of his high vantage point, holding on to the other. He placed all six of the primed sticks of dynamite beside his left hand and tossed the lit fuse high into the air.

Even his old eyes could see the flaring fuse as it fell down the ridge face and landed amid the boulders below.

But it was the hysterical sound of the twelve shocked voices which were music to his ears.

They had been frightened into giving their positions away by the sight of a burning dynamite fuse landing in their ranks. For all Smith and his gang knew, there was a stick of dynamite attached to it.

At least half the outlaws reacted exactly the way Tomahawk had anticipated and started firing their rifles and handguns in his direction. Others seemed to be moving as far away from the smouldering fuse as possible in case it exploded.

With bullets tearing at the top of the ridge sending debris all over his prostrate body, Tomahawk lifted the first stick of dynamite off the ground. He gently lowered its short fuse into the burning path of the lighted spare one and waited.

Once it had ignited, the old man hurled the explosive with deadly venom at one of the blazing rifle barrels.

Tomahawk's judgement of how long the trimmed

fuse-wire would take to burn down to the dynamite stick had been totally wrong. Less than five seconds after leaving Tomahawk's skilled right hand, the dynamite exploded.

The brilliant blinding flash and accompanying violent ear-splitting noise echoed all around the vast cattle range.

It had reached its target.

The muffled groan of Tomahawk's first victim filled the night air as Porter Bruce and his mount were blown into a half-dozen pieces.

'They got Porter, Billy Bob,' Elmer screamed in shock as he realized that he had been splattered in the blood of his cousin.

'Dynamite!' Smith snarled. 'That's why Adams stole it all from Red River.'

'What we gonna do?' Kermit called across to his elder brother.

'Open up with everything ya got, boys!' came the reply.

Faster than any man of his age ought to have been able to move, Tomahawk rolled across the rocky ground and ducked back behind the largest boulder on the very top of the ridge. He had heard the anger of his unseen enemy and knew that they had spotted him.

Now every one of their weapons were trained on where they knew he was hiding. A deafening volley of shots rained on his position. The old-timer pressed his back against the rock and watched as red-hot bullet-tapers cut through the air above his head.

'Reckon I must have upset them critters a tad,' Tomahawk muttered to himself as he endured their first direct assault on him.

For more than three solid minutes there was no let-up in the volley of deadly lead.

Tomahawk knew exactly why they were keeping him pinned down under a constant onslaught of bullet fire. They were trying to stop him from repeating his first lethal attack as they tried desperately to ascend the steep ridge.

With his heart racing the old man lit another fuse and then tossed the stick of dynamite over his head. He waited for the explosion.

He did not have to wait long.

The boulder behind Tomahawk's back shook when the dynamite blew. The oldest Bar 10 cowboy could hear the sickening sound of horses whinnying in a mixture of pain and terror far below him. The gunfire seemed to stop for what felt like an eternity and Tomahawk used the opportunity to repeat his actions.

This time the dynamite had barely left his hand. It had travelled a mere forty feet through the air when it exploded.

Outlaws were screaming for a multitude of reasons now. But these were not the cries of men who had been destroyed by the explosives, only those of the witnesses to the carnage. Mason Pyle had seen the second stick land a mere yard in front of him. It had been the last thing the outlaw would ever see. Elmer Bruce had joined his cousin in Hell when the third dynamite stick exploded above his head, turning it and most of his upper body to pulp.

The Red River Raiders had been hit and hit hard.

A quarter of their number had already been destroyed and the survivors wanted revenge.

They also wanted the old cowboy dead before he was able to claim even more of them with his dynamite.

Tomahawk raised himself on to his feet and placed his axe in his belt. He picked up the last three sticks of explosives and lit their fuses, one by one.

Like the marksman he had always been, Tomahawk hurled the first two lethal sticks down the ridge towards the sound of the infuriated voices, defying the bullets that were being fired back at him. But the remaining outlaws had scattered with their horses well away from where they had noticed all the primed dynamite sticks were landing.

With the two massive explosions that followed within seconds of one another the entire side of the ridge was bathed in light. A light that not only illuminated the Red River Raiders but also the defiant old man high above them.

Billy Bob Smith and his remaining gang were now well away from where Tomahawk had aimed his explosives. Holstering his Colt, the outlaw leader dragged his Winchester from its saddle scabbard and released his grip on his mount's reins. With a speed honed over most of his adult life, Smith cranked the rifle's mechanism and fired at the thin figure of Tomahawk.

Just as Tomahawk had lit the fuse of the last dynamite stick he felt the bullet hitting him high on his right shoulder. He reeled around with the sheer force of the bullet's impact. The old man had experienced pain countless times during his long life but nothing like this. He staggered backwards and then realized he had dropped the deadly stick of dynamite.

Tomahawk tried to regain his balance for long enough to figure out where the lit stick had gone. Then he spotted its smouldering fuse disappearing into a crack just behind his feet.

Moving like a man at least a third of his actual age, Tomahawk ran for cover.

They ground erupted violently beneath his boots. Tomahawk felt himself being lifted off the rocky surface of the ridge and then thrown into the air. Tomahawk felt branches snapping as he hurtled down through trees and bushes. Then the thin old man disappeared into a deep gully close to the line shack as rubble came cascading down over him.

Ten minutes later the remaining nine Red River Raiders rode their injured mounts up the trail and over the now silent ridge.

Billy Bob Smith slowed his horse and studied the shattered rocks where Tomahawk's last stick of dynamite had exploded.

'Reckon the bastard blew himself up with that last stick, boys.' The outlaw laughed as he led the eight remaining riders down into the land illuminated by the distant fire.

They had entered the Bar 10.

TWENTY-ONE

The sun was just rising. Monstrous flames of the raging fire were now licking at the air within the wide pass. Gene Adams and Johnny Puma tried to shield themselves from the unbearable heat as they worked. Both men moved along the sides of the pass pushing the primed dynamite sticks into every natural crevice and fault in the rockface that they could find. They had divided the explosives equally between them, fifteen sticks each, to be placed on each side of the blisteringly hot gap between the high walls of the rocky bluff.

They had to work fast because they only had five minutes to complete the job and then ride away before the first dynamite stick exploded.

Adams and Johnny knew that the fuses were five-minute ones and they had lit each one just before placing it into the rocks. So by the time the pair of exhausted men had placed the last of their lethal charges into position, they had only a matter of thirty or so seconds to reach their mounts and ride.

This was not the sort of job that either of the

cattlemen were used to. They had both used dynamite before to clear the land, but had no confidence
in the deadly explosives. They were men who
rounded up longhorn steers for a living and even to
be on foot felt totally alien to the pair.

Gene Adams had placed his last stick into position
and lit its fuse when Johnny still had a few to go. The
rancher could have left his friend to finish alone but
that was not his way. He was a Texan and Texans
stood firm. He waited for the youngster to finish
placing his share of the lethal sticks, even though
every passing second meant danger.

Adams narrowed his eyes and stared along the
pass. The sheer walls of solid rock that he knew were
now like a ticking time-bomb. At any moment the
first of the dynamite sticks would erupt and spew
boulders into the air. At any time, the flames that
were now twisting their way into the pass might cause
the explosives to overheat and start blasting. Adams
rubbed the sweat from his eyes and moved closer to
his friend.

'Hurry up, Johnny,' he whispered under his breath
as if willing his companion to finish his task even
faster than possible. 'We gotta get out of here.'

Johnny struck a match and lit the last fuse. He
placed the deadly explosive at the foot of the high
bluff wall.

'C'mon, Johnny,' Adams called out.

Johnny ran towards the rancher. Then they both
aimed the tips of their high-heeled boots in the
direction of their waiting mounts.

'How long do you figure we got, Gene?' Johnny asked. He released the reins from around the tree and threw himself on to the saddle of his horse.

'Not long enough, son,' Adams replied, grabbing at his saddle horn and pulling his weary body up on to the back of his mount.

Both riders dragged their reins hard to their right and spurred the horses at exactly the same time. The nervous creatures did not require a reminder.

'Ride, Johnny. Ride like hell,' Adams yelled out to his young pal.

Johnny did not need to be told to get out of this place. He knew that they had started something that neither of them fully understood. How big an explosion was thirty sticks of dynamite, anyway? Would it do as Gene Adams hoped and bring down both sides of the high bluff walls and fill the pass with enough rocks to stop the fire from entering the rest of the Bar 10? So many unanswerable questions raced through both riders' minds as they drove their skittish cutting horses on.

The horses thundered across the flat dry ground at full gallop with their masters standing high in their stirrups. After the pair had covered less than a few hundred yards, the first of the dynamite sticks exploded in the pass behind them.

Then the noise and impact multiplied a hundredfold. Whether the rest of the fuses had burned for their full time or perhaps the first explosions had triggered a chain reaction amongst the others, neither rider could tell. All they knew for sure was that they had never heard or felt anything quite like it.

Powerful shock waves mixed with choking dust swept over the two racing horses. It felt to Adams and Johnny as if they had been hit by a hurricane. Before they could do anything to prevent it, the sheer force of the explosions lifted the horses off the ground.

Adams and Johnny went flying over their mounts' necks and their horses rolled over as if they were tumbleweed.

Somehow, the Bar 10 men managed to cling on to their reins after they had crashed heavily into the unforgivingly hard ground.

The shock waves hammered into the two men until they felt as if they had been beaten to a pulp by some invisible enemy. When the dust and smoke finally cleared, Adams was lying on his side next to his winded mount. He rubbed his eyes and gripped the reins tightly whilst he looked for his young friend.

Johnny Puma was flat out on his back coughing. He still had the reins of his horse in his hands but there was no sign of the terrified creature, only its bridle lay next to him. Johnny rolled over and blinked hard until the dust fell from his eyes and he could see Adams.

Crawling to the rancher's side, the youngster began checking the startled horse for inhuries.

'You didn't happen to see my horse anywhere around here, did ya?'

'You lost your horse, Johnny?'

'Nope, I ain't lost it. It used to be on the end of this bridle, if you recall.' Johnny shook his head. His ears were still ringing from the noise of the massive dynamite blast a few moments earlier.

Gene Adams spat the dust from his mouth and stared back at the bluff. The pass was blocked by millions of boulders.

'It worked, Johnny. We stopped the fire in its tracks.'

Johnny seemed unimpressed.

'Reckon we used enough dynamite, Gene?'

'What do you mean?'

'Where's my horse? Blown all the way to Mexico?'

Both men started to grin until they saw something off in the distance. They staggered to their feet and began to focus their gaze in the light of the new day.

'You see that?'

'I see them.'

TWENTY-TWO

All nine of the injured horsemen stopped their mounts at exactly the same time. Even at the vast distance between the riders and the violent explosions, the shock waves ripped into them. Only the rocky ridge itself seemed capable of absorbing the power that the dynamite had unleashed. The nine outlaws could taste the acrid flavour of burning in their dry mouths as they wrestled with the reins of their spooked horses.

The massive explosions half-way across the vast land that was the Bar 10 ranch were unlike anything any of them had ever witnessed before. For a few minutes the outlaws simply sat atop their horses silently and stared in utter disbelief at what their weary eyes and dust-caked ears had just experienced.

As the light of the new day traced its way across the massive ranch the huge plume of cloud was clearly visible hanging in the blue sky above the distant bluff. The smoke from the fire beyond was still rising but was totally unlike the cloud caused by the explosive charges Gene Adams and Johnny Puma had set off.

'What in tarnation was that, Billy Bob?' Waco asked the self-imposed leader of the Red River Raiders.

'Reckon that was old man Adams making use of all that dynamite he stole from Red River, Waco,' Smith answered, rubbing his face in a vain attempt to rid it of the smell of death.

Caleb and Joey Smith drew their horses level with their elder brother's mount.

'What the hell did he blow up, Billy Bob?' they both asked at the same time.

Smith forced a grin. 'Whatever it was, it must have been mighty big. That was one hell of a bang, and no mistake.'

'For a man to use that much dynamite he must have been trying to wake the Devil himself.' Thaddeus Nelson spat at the ground with an inner rage he had seldom managed to hide from anyone who ever encountered him.

'Nelson's right,' Waco piped up. 'Adams must have gone plumb loco.'

'Or he might have been trying to stop that fire in its tracks, boys.' Billy Bob Smith nodded as his eyes managed to focus at last on the distant scene.

'With dynamite?' Tom Hetty questioned loudly.

'How can you stop a fire with explosives, Billy Bob?' Silas Jackson asked, moving his mount next to Hetty. 'Don't seem like it's possible to me.'

'Nor me.' Hetty agreed with his friend.

Smith allowed his horse to edge forward until its hoofs were balanced on a massive flat boulder. He screwed up his eyes and stared hard at the distant scene. He had heard a lot about this Bar 10 ranch over the years but it did not look anything like he had imagined it would. There were no cattle to be seen, nor cowboys for that matter, from their high vantage point. Just miles and miles of dry grass.

Smith gritted his teeth. 'It don't seem logical to me either but I'd bet a new hat that that fire ain't coming no further west any more. If'n you look real hard, you can see where it burned up everything behind it.'

'Billy Bob's right.' Kermit pointed a gloved finger at the smoke. 'I see the black ground behind the flames and there's a wall of rocks or something in front of it.'

'Can you see anyone out there, boys?' Smith asked his followers.

'I can.' Nelson nodded.

'Where?' Smith turned to stare at the one-eyed outlaw.

Thaddeus Nelson pointed. 'Two men right in front of that cloud of dust.'

Billy Bob Smith moved his horse around on the dusty ridge until he had a clear view of where Nelson was indicating with his trigger-finger.

'You can see two men down there?'

'Yep,' Nelson replied.

Smith shrugged. He had no idea whether the older rider was right or wrong. He simply could not see as well with his two eyes as Nelson could with his one. 'If'n you say there are two men there, then I figure there must be.'

'That was one hell of a big explosion.' Broncho Bates muttered under his breath. 'I ain't never seen its like before and that's a fact.'

'You just woke up, Broncho?' Smith snapped at the big outlaw.

Bates sighed. Big as he was, he would not go up against the oldest Smith brother however much he taunted him.

'My ears are ringing like it's a Sunday-go-to-meeting day,' Waco grumbled.

'You figure it was Adams that blew up that dynamite?' Caleb asked his elder and wiser brother.

'It was Adams, OK.' Billy Bob Smith sank his spurs into the flesh of his horse and forced it to continue down the hill towards the Bar 10 pastures. 'I know it was Adams.'

'Where do ya figure he is now?'

Smith looked over his shoulder at the riders who were trailing him faithfully.

'I figure he must be one of the two bastards Nelson reckons are down there. Let's go kill us a rich old man, boys.'

TWENTY-THREE

Bar 10 wrangler Larry Drake drove his sorrel mare hard like the expert horseman that he was. The rider had been stuck out at the southernmost region of the huge cattle ranch for nearly three weeks with fellow cowboy Hank Weaver. They had not been called upon to help fight the fire, they had a more important job to do.

Larry had seen the distant flames rising all the previous night even from their remote line shack but it had only been when the earth shook beneath the hoofs of his horse in response to the explosion in the pass, that he decided to act.

The young cowboy spurred his horse on as the first rays of sun swept across the Bar 10.

Drawn like a moth to a naked flame, the wrangler headed his mare north for the ranch house, where he felt he might find answers to the questions that filled his mind. Until the first in the series of blasts had rocked the Bar 10, Larry had been trying to keep what was left of Gene Adams's remaining stock

129

contained in the safer pastures. The explosion had been so powerful and unexpected that he had been blown from his Texan saddle like a rag-doll. As the centre of the cattle spread was closer than returning to the remote southern outpost, Larry had decided to ride north to try and find out what was going on.

Never a curious soul by nature, it was strange for the young wrangler to feel drawn to investigate anything. But seeing and feeling the massive blast had been something that even he could not resist.

The legs of the sturdy cutting horse ate up the ground beneath the determined cowboy. He had already covered more than five miles when, gallop-ing along a seldom-used trail at the bottom of a hundred-foot high mesa, Larry caught sight of the dry panorama ahead of him. It was hard to believe that this was the Bar 10 ranch at all. He slapped his long reins across the shoulders of his lathered-up mare and urged it onward.

Arriving at a flat stretch of pastureland which was usually green with lush grass that reached the bellies of the ranch's famed longhorn steers, the rider hauled in his reins and tried to get his bearings. The grass was brown and sparse and made the entire landscape appear different from when he had last ridden through it a mere three weeks earlier.

Only the smoke from the now-contained fire beyond the bluff gave him reason to accept that he was where he thought he was. The tall funnel of pulverized-stone dust still hung in the air above the pass.

Larry stood in his stirrups and slapped his horse with the ends of his reins once more. The mare thundered on at breakneck speed across the dusty ground towards where he assumed the trail to the ranch house must be.

Gene Adams and Johnny Puma had been walking the winded horse for almost a mile when they spotted the dust rising directly to the south. Both men felt the palms of their hands stroking the grips of their Colt .45s.

'You see that, Gene?' Johnny asked the older man uneasily.

'Yep. I seen it five minutes back,' Adams drawled, pulling the brim of his black ten-gallon hat down to shield his eyes from the bright morning light.

'Who is it?'

'It must be either Hank or Larry,' Adams replied.

Johnny gave a huge sigh of relief. 'For a minute there I thought it must be one of them riders we spotted coming through the trail over the western ridge.'

'I doubt that, son.' Adams patted the shoulder of the young cowboy reassuringly.

'Reckon you're right, Gene. It must be either Larry or Hank coming to take themselves a look at what's been going on.'

'As long as one of them is still looking after them steers of ours, I don't mind,' Adams said bluntly.

'Which one is it?' Johnny asked, trying to identify the galloping rider.

Adams stopped walking and held on to the nose of the skittish horse as he watched the rider closing in on them at terrific speed.

'By the way that cowboy is pushing that sorrel, I'd say it was Larry.'

Johnny nodded in agreement. 'Yeah, Hank would have fallen off his horse at half that speed.'

'Hank's a good man. He just tends to let a little too much daylight between his saddle and his britches.' Adams smiled.

Larry seemed to be riding well away from the two men when he spotted them waving their Stetsons. He turned his galloping mount in their direction and raced towards them.

Dust rose over the two men when Larry hauled his mare to a complete halt.

'What's going on, boys?' Larry asked the pair of dust-caked men. 'What was that explosion?'

'It's a long story,' Adams replied. 'Where's Hank?'

'He stayed in the line shack whilst I went tending the steers, Gene.' Larry rubbed his face along the back of his sleeve.

Adams shook his head and pointed to the distant western ridge.

'Can you see them riders, Larry?'

'Nine of the critters,' Larry said instantly.

'Nine?' Johnny raised an eyebrow. 'There were a dozen of them heading into Red River.'

'Maybe old Tomahawk managed to pick a few of them off.' Gene Adams's face was grim as he spoke.

Johnny felt his throat go dry. 'Tomahawk was

meant to stop them from entering the Bar 10, Gene. I just had me a thought that don't sit well in my craw.'

'Yep, Johnny.' Adams placed a hand on the cowboy's shoulder. 'It means that they got past the old scarecrow.'

'They'd have had to kill him to do that, Gene.' Johnny's voice cracked as the words left his lips.

'Yep. I reckon you're right, son.'

'No, Gene,' Johnny protested.' Tomahawk can't be dead.'

'They'd have had to kill him to get on to the Bar 10, Johnny.'

Larry Drake licked his lips, then spoke.

'You figure Tomahawk is dead?'

Gene Adams stared up at the rider. He said nothing. His troubled face did not require words to confirm his worst fears for his oldest pal.

'Who are those varmints, Gene?' Larry asked.

'A pretty bad bunch,' Adams told him. 'Call themselves the Red River Raiders, Larry.'

Larry stood in his stirrups and narrowed his eyes.

'You lost a horse, boys?'

'Yep. We did.' Adams nodded.

'I think I found him.' Larry untied his rope from his saddle horn and made a long loop before urging his horse on.

Adams and Johnny watched as their friend raced across the dry ground swinging his cutting rope above his head.

'What we gonna do, Gene?' asked Johnny.

Adams stared out to the distant western ridge. The

riders must have reached the foot of the tall rocky incline because he could no longer see them.

'We're gonna fight, son.'

TWENTY-FOUR

The Red River Raiders could almost taste their new-found wealth as they rode deeper and deeper into the Bar 10. As far as they were concerned, this was their land now. They had fought to enter its sacred boundaries and won. For more than three hours they had seen nothing more frightening than a few jack rabbits and they were growing in confidence with every stride of their mounts' long legs. Where was the famous Gene Adams who, it was said, ruled this country like a medieval monarch?

Had Adams given up the ghost and finally bowed out in the presence of better men? The nine brutal killers all thought that he must have.

Otherwise he would have been waiting for them with a deadly reception committee.

But there was no one here to halt their progress. Billy Bob Smith could hardly believe their luck. It had seemed totally insane to even consider entering the Bar 10 when they were back in Red River but now they were actually riding through its valleys unhindered and unchallenged.

Adams was gone.

The Bar 10 was, to all intents and purposes, theirs. They had dared and they had conquered.

The prize was theirs.

They had taken a million acres of prime cattle-rearing land in the heart of Texas at the cost of only three of their intrepid force. They knew it ought to have been harder but they were not grumbling. It had been so very, very easy. As the nine horsemen steered their mounts closer and closer to the heart of the ranch they began to wonder why no one had ever tried to take on Adams before.

They had faced one man with spirit back on the ridge and then there had been no further resistance to their invasion.

Nothing could stop them now.

The sky above the Bar 10 was angry. But not as angry as the three horsemen who had driven their mounts across its vast open ranges to reach its very heart. Gene Adams led Johnny and Larry into the courtyard of the Bar 10 at a pace that echoed the utter determination of the trio. They dismounted quickly and allowed their mounts to find their own way to the water hole near the corrals.

'C'mon, boys!' Adams ran towards the ranch house with his two companions on his heels.

Once inside the cool interior of the building, the

rancher and his two men moved across the huge living-room and into the study where Gene kept all the weaponry and ammunition for the Bar 10.

Adams opened the top drawer of his hand-carved desk, took out a key-ring and tossed it into Johnny's hands. He pointed at the gun-rack on the wall.

'Break out them rifles, Johnny.'

Johnny unlocked the padlock that secured a chain laced through the gleaming hand guards of the Winchester rifles.

'Why do we need all these rifles, Gene? There's only three of us.'

Adams opened a wall cabinet filled with ammunition and removed several boxes of cartridges of varying calibres. He stacked them on the green leather top of his desk in neat piles.

'I figure that we'll need every one of them before this day is much older, Johnny.'

Larry Drake helped Johnny to pull the Winchester rifles off the wall rack and place them across the arms of a well-padded armchair.

'We gonna load all these carbines, Gene?'

'Every single one of them, Larry,' Adams replied.

'But why?' Johnny asked, dropping the last rifle on top of the others. 'A man can only use one rifle. There are twenty or more here.'

Adams looked up at the youthful face.

'One rifle at a time, son. We can use one rifle at a time.'

Johnny suddenly began to understand his friend's intentions.

'I get it. This way we don't have to waste time reloading our rifles if we get pinned down.'

'Exactly, Johnny.' Adams picked up two boxes of .45 bullets and tossed one to the cowboy. 'Fill your pockets with bullets for them Colts of yours and then start loading the rifles. We ain't got much time if my figuring is right. They gotta be darn close by now.'

'You figure them Red River Raiders are heading here, Gene?' Larry asked fearfully.

'Yep. They're coming here OK, Larry.' Adams glanced out of the window and stared to the west. He could already see dust rising beyond the line of trees which edged the courtyard of his beloved Bar 10 ranch.

'How can you be so sure, Gene?' Johnny asked as he filled his pockets with the bullets for his matched pair of Colt .45s.

Gene Adams pulled the lace drape aside and rubbed at the dirt on the window pane.

'Mainly because I can see their dust about a mile off, Johnny.'

Beneath an angry large black cloud that slowly edged its way over the million acres of the Bar 10, Billy Bob Smith drew in his reins and studied the sight before them with a relish not common in his sort. He was looking at the very soul of the ranch and knew it was now within his grasp. Less than a mile below their vantage point on the dusty rise, the very centre of the richest cattle spread in Texas just lay lifelessly waiting for him and his men to strike.

Smith felt like a diamond-back rattler waiting for the exact moment to sink its venomous fangs into its unsuspecting prey.

The rest of the Red River Raiders circled their horses next to their pensive leader and waited for him to speak.

'You see them three horses roaming around in that courtyard, boys?' Smith asked.

'We see 'em, Billy Bob.' Waco sighed. 'But I ain't likely to get excited by a few nags.'

'Them horses have been ridden hard,' Smith added.

'So?' Kermit piped up. 'Our horses ain't exactly fresh if'n you'd bother to look a tad closer.'

The eldest of the Smith brothers slapped Kermit around the back of his ear and pointed at the horses again. 'So it means that their riders must be in or around the house or outbuildings, Kerm.'

'I thought you said that Adams and his men had lit out.' Joey looked hard at his older brother.

'I said that, didn't I? That don't alter the fact that someone's down there though. Could be Adams or maybe it's just a few of his hands looking for grub or the like.' Billy Blob Smith pulled a cigar from his vest pocket and tore the end of it with his teeth. 'I figure they're in the house.'

'How come?' Nelson tilted his head and gazed at Smith with his one good eye. It was an unnerving sight to the uninitiated.

' 'Coz that's where I'd be if'n I had the choice, Thaddeus,' Smith growled.

Nelson shrugged. 'You could be right.'

'What's our next move?' Broncho Bates asked as a heavenly noise echoed eerily above them and forked lightning flashed around the edges of the black cloud which now seemed to fill the entire sky above the Bar 10.

Smith struck a match across his saddle horn and cupped its flame to the tip of his cigar. He inhaled the strong smoke and brooded for a few moments.

'We're going in cautious. We already lost three of our band and I ain't about to add to that score.'

'You want me to scout the situation out, Billy Bob?' Caleb asked.

Smith nodded and watched as his youngest brother teased his horse down towards the rear of the large barn. His eyes stared heavenward as he heard the distant rumbling of thunder again above them.

'There's a storm brewing, boys.'

Billy Bob Smith had no idea how right he was.

TWENTY-FIVE

Caleb Smith had learned a lot by being the youngest member of the notorious Smith clan. He had learned how to kill and how not to get himself killed. He had also learned that he was probably the most expendable member of the deadly gang. He was not as good with either his guns or his rifle as they were and knew that to remain part of the Raiders he had to excel at something that none of his brothers or fellow outlaws cared to do. He had chosen to be their advance guard.

Their scout.

Their scapegoat.

For most of his days since he had first joined Billy Bob and the rest of the Red River Raiders it had been his job to check out dangerous situations before the rest of the outlaws risked their lives. It had been Caleb who had been sent into the sleepy town of Red River ahead of Billy Bob and when satisfied that all was well, he had signalled for the remainder of the gang to join him. He knew his place in the chain of command.

He was expendable. Over the past decade he had narrowly escaped death eleven times and been wounded only once.

Caleb slid from his saddle behind the Bar 10 barn and moved like a panther through the empty building until he could see directly into the large ranch house opposite.

For a few moments Caleb saw nothing. The outlaw knew that the house was probably the place where the masters of the three horses were, just as Billy Bob had said. Holstering one of his pistols, Caleb walked cautiously away from the huge open doorway of the barn back into the dark shadows. He stared up into the hay loft and then began to climb the fixed wooden ladder. When he reached the loft, he crawled to the open window and stared down at Gene Adams's home. Within a few beats of his heart he spotted the figures moving inside the study of the house.

They were there just as his eldest sibling had said. Caleb stood up and gazed out across the half-mile distance between the courtyard and the awaiting Red River Raiders. He waved his Stetson above his head several times before Billy Bob returned the signal. Before the outlaw had knelt back down amid the hay, he had seen the eight riders spurring their horses and heading in after him.

Hetty and Jackson led the troop of riders down through the dry brush towards the rear of the large wooden buildings. Billy Bob Smith rode in the centre of the Raiders, balancing his carbine on his left hip. He was ready for anything and knew that was probably what they would get dished out at them if Gene Adams was within the Bar 10 compound.

Smith dismounted first and waved Bates and Kermit to his left before sending Joey and Waco to the right. They had their orders and could be relied upon to execute them with cold-blooded expertise.

The outlaw leader checked his weaponry carefully, inhaled on what remained of his cigar, then gripping it firmly between his teeth, he marched through the interior of the barn with Nelson, Hetty and Jackson at his side. Each man carried his long rifle expertly as he had always done. They knew how to kill with many weapons but mostly they chose the long-distance impersonal method that their repeating rifles gave them.

Reaching the barn entrance the four men fanned out, two to each side of the immense doors. Smith cranked the mechanism of his Winchester and stared up at the hay loft.

'Stay there, Caleb,' he ordered.

Suddenly the entire courtyard was bathed in blinding flashing light a few seconds before the deafening noise of thunder shook the buildings. Smith hoisted his rifle to his chest as if he might be able to silence the storm with a well-placed bullet.

It was as if a dam had burst directly above them. The driving rain came down furiously. Within seconds, the entire Bar 10 was awash with water incapable of penetrating the ground, baked rock-hard after ten months of drought.

'What the hell?' Smith shouted at the sky.

Gene Adams had no idea what had caught his attention first. It might have been the sudden downpouring of much-needed rain or the screaming voice of the outlaw leader. Whatever it was, Adams had been drawn to the window again just seconds before the volley of bullets shattered the glass window panes.

Splinters of glass showered over the stunned rancher. Gene Adams dived for cover, dragging the two younger cowboys with him. They watched in horror as the pine wall of the study was torn apart by a score of bullets.

The house shook again as another massive thunderclap deafened the three cowboys inside the study.

'Reckon they must be a mite closer than you figured, Gene,' Johnny said. He brushed the glass from his shoulders and crawled to the side of the rancher who had returned to the bullet ridden wall.

'Well spotted, Johnny.' Adams pointed the golden barrel of one of his Colts through the window at the barn and fired. Even through the driving rain Adams could see the men moving away from the barn entrance as his bullet ripped a chunk out of the doorframe.

'How many are there, Gene?' Johnny asked as he too let a bullet go at the wooden building.

Larry Drake bit his lip as the sound of another

massive heavenly explosion closely followed a lighting flash.

'Reckon someone up there is a tad cranky, Gene.'

Adams squinted through the window and watched the rain lashing down against the barn and main bunkhouse.

'I see a couple of rifle barrels down at the corner of the bunkhouse, boys.'

'There's another couple of critters moving across from the barn to the back of the house, Gene.' Johnny cocked the triggers on both his .45s and fired twice, trying to stop the men in their tracks. A distant cry told him that he had winged one of them.

'You hit one of them by the sound of it, son,' Adams said.

'He kept on moving though,' Johnny said angrily knowing he had missed a golden opportunity to reduce their enemies by one.

'Easy, son. At least you hit him.' Adams glanced around the study and all the weaponry they had primed for action. 'We had better get us a better place to make a stand than here.'

'You figure we got a chance against them *hombres?*' Larry asked as he trailed the two men away from the window towards the pile of rifles.

'Not if we stay in here, Larry,' Adams replied, taking an armful of the Winchester rifles and moving out into the large living-room. 'The walls ain't thick enough.'

The two younger cowboys carried the remainder of the rifles out into the big room as another volley of rifle bullets tore their way through the wooden walls of the study behind them.

'See what ya mean, Gene.' Larry gulped.

'Where we gonna make a stand, Gene?' Johnny asked the rancher. 'We can't get out of here. They got us trapped in this house.'

Gene Adams laid the heavy bundle of rifles on top of the table and edged his way to the open door. He glanced across at the bunkhouse and barn. The distance between the buildings was now like a river as the rain continued to fall relentlessly.

'If this rain makes it hard for us to see them, I figure they have the same problem, boys,' Adams said, cocking his gun hammer and firing again.

The shot was returned tenfold.

Bullets bounced off the ranch house door-frame sending splinters cascading over the tall rancher. Adams drew back and stared at his two troubled companions.

'Reckon we are pinned down at that.'

'You mean that we're stuck in this house whilst them killers are out there taking pot-shots at us?' Johnny dropped his rifles on to the table next to the ones Adams had left there.

Adams gritted his teeth and rubbed his gloved left hand over his chin. The rain came thundering down even harder making it virtually impossible to see anything further than a few feet from the house.

'I don't like it much myself, boys.'

'I ain't much of a gunfighter, Gene.' Larry sighed.

Adams glanced across at the wrangler.

'Just duck when the shooting starts up again, Larry. Johnny and me will do the tricky stuff with the guns.'

Larry wondered how the rancher could manage to wink when they were facing almost certain death.

'This is serious ain't it, Gene?'

Adams smiled. 'That all depends.'

'On what?'

'On how eager they are to fight or maybe die.'

TWENTY-SIX

Kermit Smith rested his back against the rear wall of the ranch house and felt as if he had just been kicked by a mule. As rain poured over him he felt the agonizing wound in his side. Blood was pouring from the bullet hole he had just discovered. The huge figure of Broncho Bates realized that his companion was not winded, he was dying.

'You're hit, Kerm,' Bates said, holding on to the shoulders of the outlaw as he slid down into the mud at his feet. The wall of the house was covered in blood.

Kermit managed to look up into the face of his worried friend before his eyes rolled back and he fell lifeless on to the large muddy boots.

Broncho Bates eyes widened. One of Billy Bob's brothers had just died. That was something that filled the big man with terror. How would the outlaw leader react when he discovered the news?

Bates stood to his full six foot three and leaned on the side wall. He could see the exchange of bullets between the house and the barn continuing through the torrential downpour.

'Billy Bob!' Bates finally shouted across at Smith's blazing Winchester. 'Billy Bob! Kerm's been killed.'

Suddenly the shooting from the side of the bunkhouse and the barn ceased. There was a long chilling silence that froze the huge Bates to the spot. He knew the eldest Smith could become a monster if things did not go as he planned. What would he do when faced with something as unthinkable as losing one of his kin?

The figure of Billy Bob Smith came from around the side of the barn and raced across the flooded distance between the two buildings. He stopped at Bates's side and looked down at his lifeless brother Kermit.

'You let them kill my brother?' Smith's voice muttered under his breath.

Bates knew better than to say anything when Smith was like this. It could prove fatal even to look into the crazed eyes of the outlaw when he was angry. He looked away from the probing eyes until he felt the man brush past him.

'Adams did this, Broncho.'

'They was shooting at us, Billy Bob.'

Smith stepped to the corner of the house and called out to his men. There was an insanity in the raised voice which every one of them recognized.

'C'mon, you lazy bastards. There are only three of them.'

Reluctantly the outlaws all obeyed the command

of Billy Bob Smith and stepped out into the ceaseless rain with their rifles cocked and readied in their hands.

Each man fired with every step he took as they closed in on the Bar 10 ranch house. They knew that they were facing the deadly guns of the famed rancher and his two men in what seemed an almost suicidal attack. Yet they feared Billy Bob Smith far more than they did any faceless rancher. The wrath of Smith was something none of the Red River Raiders seemed capable of facing sober.

The blinding rain was the outlaws' only shield. They all hoped it was capable of protecting them from their foolhardy onslaught. Gene Adams and Johnny Puma seemed to question their own eyesight when they saw the six men boldly marching directly towards them firing their rifles.

'Rifles, Larry,' Adams called to the wrangler behind them.

Larry Drake tossed two fully loaded Winchesters into the hands of Adams and Johnny. Both men swung around, cocked and fired their deadly carbines at the approaching men.

Bullets peppered the large room in reply to the Bar 10 men's defensive shots. Shafts of wood and sawdust showered over the two cowboys as they blasted their rifles again and again.

Waco fell into the mud almost unnoticed by the rest of the battling outlaws. Gunsmoke was washed away instantly as it left the barrels of the rifles. Only Joey Smith stopped to see if Waco was still alive.

The bullets that tore into his young body forced him backwards. Joey lay in the foot-deep water trying to work out how badly injured he was. He had no idea he was already as good as dead.

One-eyed Thaddeus Nelson had tried to move faster than the others across the distance between the two buildings. But he had not bargained for the mud that was almost quicksand. Finding one boot sucked from his foot, he made the error of trying to retrieve it. Nelson died instantly.

Finding their rifles empty, Tom Hetty and Silas Jackson moved closer together as they discarded the Winchesters and drew their four Colts. Both men cocked and fired their pistols in neat carefully practised actions.

It was Jackson who was hit first in the shoulder and found himself on his knees. The tall man lurched forward and watched as his two guns in his gloved hands disappeared into the mud. Hetty continued firing whilst pulling his friend back to his feet.

With more bullets whizzing through the blinding rain at the outlaws, Jackson raised his guns and squeezed both their triggers.

The blocked barrels of Jackson's pistols caused one to misfire and the other to explode. Both men reeled backwards when Adams and Johnny Puma managed to find their targets. Hetty and Jackson landed together in the mud. They were in death, as they always were in life, together.

Having had to climb down from the hay loft of the barn, Caleb Smith had been the last of the Red River

Raiders to leave the building. He could hardly see anything but the flashes of gunfire before him and the forked lightning above. Forcing his way through the rain with his rifle clutched firmly in his hands, the youngest of the Smiths tripped over the almost submerged body of Waco.

The terrified outlaw wallowed in the mud, desperately trying to find his rifle as bullets tore into him from the barrels of both Johnny and Adams's Winchesters. He fell face first into the deep water. There were no bubbles. He had breathed his last.

Gene Adams tossed the empty rifle away and accepted a new fully loaded weapon as he brushed the sawdust from his face.

Johnny gestured to Larry. The wrangler threw him a fresh repeating rifle to replace his empty one.

'How many were there to start with, Gene?'

Adams raised a gloved finger to his lips as he tried to listen out for more of their attackers. The rumbling storm and the merciless rain made hearing anything outside the house impossible.

'We must have killed them all by now, surely?' Johnny questioned the rancher.

Adams shook his head.

'Two or three of them went around towards the back of the house, Johnny.'

Johnny squinted out into the rain. He could not see any signs of life amongst the outlaws who had come straight at them. But he started to think about the men who had braved his bullets and run to the side of the ranch house.

'Where do ya figure they are, Gene?'

Adams moved cautiously out on to the porch with the rifle in his hands. He could hear his own heart-beat drumming into his brain with every step. Johnny followed the tall rancher.

Even under the generous roof of the porch the two Bar 10 men were getting soaked to the skin.

Gene Adams paused at the corner of the porch and inhaled deeply. He cocked the rifle and then turned around the corner with his eyes screwed up. Johnny was looking all around the courtyard for any signs of the missing outlaws. There was none to be seen.

'Where the heck are they?' Johnny asked aloud.

Adams stepped back to the side of his young pal and was about to speak when they heard a crashing sound at the rear of the kitchen. Both men raced into the house again, where they saw the huge Broncho Bates stumbling to the floor after shoulder-ing the locked and bolted kitchen door off its hinges.

'Duck, Larry!' Adams screamed at their young friend who was in the line of fire.

Larry Drake stood open-mouthed not knowing which way to look until a bullet from Billy Bob Smith's Winchester knocked him off his feet.

Johnny Puma pushed Adams aside and fired straight into Bates before the big outlaw had a chance to get to his feet. With bullets from Smith passing over his head, Johnny discarded his rifle and drew both his matched Colts. With a speed of hands that defied anyone to actually see it, he fired both guns.

Smith hovered for a few endless seconds, then his rifle fell from his hands and he stared down at his chest. The notorious outlaw was about to speak when his face went pale.

Smith fell heavily on top of the already felled Bates. Neither man felt a thing. They had made their last mistakes.

Gene Adams stared at the ghastly scene before moving to Larry's side. He knelt and lifted the wounded cowboy up off the floor.

'Sorry, Gene,' Larry said. 'I got kinda mixed up.'

'How is he?' Johnny asked after holstering his guns.

Adams checked the wound carefully.

'He ain't ever gonna play the fiddle again but I reckon he'll live, Johnny.'

Johnny said nothing. All he could think about was Tomahawk lying up on the western ridge somewhere.

FINALE

It was a grim Gene Adams and Johnny Puma who rode up the trail on to the western ridge after the storm had ended. Both riders steered their horses up to the line shack and then dismounted.

Gene Adams stood silently looking at the debris that had been caused by Tomahawk's last dynamite stick.

'Where do you figure his body is, Gene?'

Adams frowned and started walking to where their horses were stabled at the side of the shack. Then he noticed a broken branch hanging at the side of the corral.

'What do you reckon broke that branch, Johnny?'

The young cowboy walked to the branch and bit his lower lip thoughtfully.

'I can't say, Gene.' He admitted.

Suddenly both men heard a noise down in a leafy gully next to the corral. They drew their guns swiftly and trained them on the spot.

'Could be a mountain lion,' Gene, Johnny said nervously.

Adams stared at his chestnut mare and the pinto pony as well as the other horses in the corral.

'If that was a cougar or a bear, them horses would be spooked. They ain't even troubled.'

The two men cautiously made their way down through the bushes and rubble. The sight that met their curious eyes stopped both men in their tracks.

Tomahawk was lying covered in leaves and stones. He was wet from the storm but fully conscious. He was also stuck.

'Tomahawk!' Johnny exclaimed sliding his gun back into its holster. 'You're alive!'

'What's the matter, Johnny?' Tomahawk responded. 'Ya disappointed?'

'Sure am, old-timer,' the young cowboy grinned. 'I always love a good funeral.'

Tomahawk's beard bristled. 'About time you two showed up. I've been stuck here for who knows how long.'

'How did you get down here?' Adams leaned over and gripped one of Tomahawk's arms whilst Johnny grabbed the other. Both men pulled the older man out of the gully and brushed him down. Tomahawk's face screwed up as he remembered the bullet in his shoulder.

'It weren't easy, Gene.'

'You've been winged, Tomahawk,' Johnny said looking hard at the blood-soaked shirt. 'Does it hurt?'

'Only when ya pokes it.' Tomahawk brushed his younger friend aside.

'I'm sure glad you're OK, old-timer.' Adams smiled.

Tomahawk looked at Adams.

'Did you think I was a goner too?'

'I'm afraid so, old-timer.' Adams shrugged.

Tomahawk gave a huge sigh and then clambered back up beside the shack.

'Well I'm ready.'

'Ready for what?' Johnny asked.

'To get the rest of them Red River Raiders.' Tomahawk slapped his right fist into the palm of his left hand. 'Come on, boys. I'll show them what's what. I'll pulverize the varmints. Tear them limb from limb.'

Gene Adams rested his hands on the bony shoulders of his oldest friend and smiled into the twinkling eyes.

'It's all over, Tomahawk. We beat the tar out of them already. They're all dead.'

Tomahawk raised both his eyebrows.

'You beat them without me to help you?'

'Yep, we did.' Johnny laughed.

'Impossible!' The old man shook his head, ambled to the corral and rested his arms on the fence poles.

Gene Adams tugged at Tomahawk's beard. 'It wasn't easy but we managed somehow.'

'Mind you I did soften the critters up before they got to you boys.' Tomahawk's eyes glinted in the late afternoon sun.

Gene Adams smiled and looked down on his ranch. The rain had returned and probably saved their lives in more ways than one, he thought.

'Let's take this old scarecrow home, Johnny,' Adams said as he noticed a rainbow arcing its way over the heart of the Bar 10 far below them. 'We got us some celebrating to do.'